Chapter 1

I ran for my life down the corridor. My lungs strained as I gasped for air. Behind me people were shouting at me, but all I could hear was my pulse pounding in my head.

Curious onlookers—little old ladies, schoolkids, mothers with strollers—stepped quickly out of my path as I zigged and zagged like a ricocheting bullet.

I knew I was breaking the law. In fact, I even knew which one. I was in violation of municipal code 11:14.4, disruption of commerce in a public place. In English, I was hauling butt right through our town mall's back-to-school sale.

In the suit and tie that my mom made me wear, I looked like an escapee from a Catholic

1

boys' school. People watched me as if they half expected to see a nun zoom by in hot pursuit. I jumped over a bench and glanced down at my watch. 4:45. Fifteen minutes to go. *I might not make it.*

A stocky kid in glasses chugged along behind me: Bentley Ellerbee, my friend since first grade, all four feet, six inches of him. I was a little bit faster, but that wasn't saying much. Even on a good day Bentley was in no danger of being nicknamed the Gazelle.

"Would you slow down?" he yelled, panting. "You're going to get us both killed!"

"I said I'd be there at seventeen hundred hours," I yelled over my shoulder, sounding just like a cop. "I don't want to be late."

"So what if you're late?" Bentley asked, struggling to keep up. "It's your birthday! He'll wait!"

"You don't know my stepdad," I replied.

Bentley and I had spent the day looking at store displays at the mall. Well, I guess drooling is closer to it. Bentley's birthday wasn't until November, in three months, but he was already planning his wish list. He had his eye on a big Meade telescope—"4.5-inch lens, f-8, equatorial mount with a motor drive," Bentley told me, as if I'd have any idea what he meant. Bentley is our town science fiction expert, so he takes his telescopes very seriously.

I was hoping for a professional camera. I figured until I was old enough to go to a real shooting range, I'd get a good workout shooting photographs. If I worked hard at it, maybe I'd be made an auxiliary police photographer—take pictures of crime scenes, evidence, even give testimony in court.

The camera I had in mind was expensive because of all the extra features I'd need: a supertelephoto lens, an infrared strobe, a computer interface so I could e-mail my photos to the FBI if they needed to put out an all-points bulletin. The price tag didn't worry me, though. If there's one thing you could say for my parents, it was that they knew how to spend money on me. My home was the only one I knew where gifts were exchanged on Groundhog Day.

But that was the problem. Sometimes it seemed as if my parents thought that if they spent the *money* on me, they didn't have to spend *time* with me. Most of my friends wonder why I even care. They tell me they'd be thrilled if their parents stopped talking to them, period. I guess it's different when your parents barely ever talk to you at all.

Here I was, at the dawn of my teen years, and I still didn't know what it was like to have a family like most kids. My first dad walked out on us when I was four years old, before I was old enough to remember him. After that, Mom was always at work, trying to make ends meet. I don't have any brothers or sisters, so I grew up alone.

My stepdad, Donald, married my mom six years ago, but I still feel as though I've just met him. He made a lot of money as the vice president of a big corporation. I barely ever saw him because he was always planning a deal or away on a business trip.

My mom . . . well, my mom has never been the same since my first dad left. I think I remind her of him—I have the same blue eyes and black hair, the same lopsided smile. But I guess I also remind her that he's gone. When she thinks about him, it makes her so sad that I figure she'd rather not see me at all.

I vaulted over an End of Summer cardboard display and hit the ground running. The doors of the mall were only a few feet away. I reached out my hand to push through, bracing myself against the impact. But instead of hitting the doors, I went careening head-first as they were swiftly pulled open mere inches in front of me.

"This way, Your Majesty," a voice snickered.

I stumbled, but I didn't fall. I managed to catch my balance and spin around.

A redheaded kid stood holding the door open with one hand. He held a skateboard in the other.

It was Jack Raynes, our class clown. Class idiot was more like it. I was the frequent target of his lamebrained insults. He thought it was pretty funny that my mom made me wear a tie. He made sure I knew it, too.

"I don't have time for you, Jack," I said. "I'm late."

"Places to go, people to see?" he inquired, batting his eyelashes. "You know, I've been meaning to ask you: Where *do* you buy your cuff links? I need a dozen."

Just then Bentley appeared in the doorway, wheezing heavily.

"Hey, Bentley," Jack said, "what's the cutoff for midgets these days? You'd know, right?"

"Shut . . . up, Jack," Bentley squeaked in

between pants. "I'm about . . . to hit . . . a growth spurt."

"Sure," Jack asked. "I bet by the time you're sixteen, you hit five foot."

"Come on, Bentley," I said, heading for the bicycle rack. I knew Jack was just after attention, so I decided not to give him any.

"You have to leave?" Jack cried, clutching his heart. "I'm crushed!"

"Under a truck, I hope," Bentley muttered, straddling his bike.

"Let's go," I said, hopping onto my B.M.X. Together Bentley and I wheeled out on the road.

"Remember his name, ladies and gentlemen!" Jack called after us. "There goes the best-dressed boy in Metier, Wisconsin. Todd Aldridge!"

I waved good-bye to Bentley from the driveway and raced into the garage. I was damp with perspiration—it was about a hundred degrees out—but I was going to make it in time.

Don's Lexus was still in its space. So was Mom's Volvo. A good sign. I relaxed—

And that was my mistake.

6

For as I stepped out of the garage into the laundry room something huge and hairy lunged at me out of the shadows. I caught the glint of fangs, the flash of its eyes just before it tackled me to the ground, its foul breath hot against my neck.

For as I stepped out of the grove, into the timmy room something huge and hairy lunged at me out of the shadows. I caught the great dog, the flash of its teeth just before it rushed me to the ground its feral breath hot against my neck.

_____ **Chapter 2**

"Max!" I yelled as the monster playfully licked my face. "Max! Down, boy! I'm in a hurry!"

I had wanted a German shepherd, which is the official police dog, but luckily Mom had insisted on a golden retriever. Of all dog breeds I think they are the friendliest and most loyal. It was hard to believe that the happy, shaggy beast crouching over me was the same small golden creature I once held in the palm of my hand.

I had been training Max to be a guard dog his whole life, and it was finally starting to pay off. He was already pretty good at "sneak attack." Next I was going to teach him to track a scent like a bloodhound. By the time I was ready for high school, I figured he'd be ready to sniff out bombs. "Don't let that animal in here," said my mother as I stepped into the cool air-conditioning of the kitchen.

She was standing by the kitchen table, where Donald was seated with a newspaper. He had stopped reading the financial section and was staring at his pocket watch.

"Four fifty-nine," he pronounced, clicking its gold cover shut. "Right on time. You're either going to grow up to be a train conductor or a watchmaker."

"Or the chief of the FBI," I said.

"Stop teasing him, Don," my mother said. She took in my suit, dark with perspiration and covered in blond dog hairs. She frowned. "Oh, Todd. You're a mess!"

"If my regulation summer uniform weren't a wool suit," I said, working a finger beneath my sticky collar, "I'd be a much *neater* mess."

"Now, now, let's not be talking back to our mother on our birthday," Don said sharply. "Why don't you hurry up and get showered and changed. We've got a big night ahead of us."

I ran up the stairs to my room, struggling out of my damp suit jacket and yanking off my tie as I went. I looked at my reflection in my mirror as

I headed for the bathroom. The sight wasn't pleasing.

When was I going to start sprouting some muscles? I was going to turn thirteen in a matter of hours, and I still looked like the Human Twig. If things didn't change soon, by the time I became a cop, I'd have no problem catching criminals— they'd probably laugh themselves unconscious just looking at me.

Inches from entering the shower, I stopped short. Sure, I was sweaty. Sure, I was smelly. But I knew that the more time I spent getting ready, the more chance there was that Don would get a call from the office. And if that happened, I could kiss my birthday evening good-bye.

I sniffed my armpits . . . and reeled from the shock. Well, I decided, I would just keep upwind from any innocent bystanders. I slapped on some deodorant and ran back into my room, keeping my ears pricked for the sound of Don's cell phone or his pager.

What was I going to wear? Mom probably wanted me in another suit. But it was *my* birthday, not hers. I grabbed my favourite faded green T-shirt and jeans and stepped into a pair of Teva sandals. So far, no phone call.

5:05. I was about to head downstairs when I

stopped myself short. They were going to know I hadn't showered. I needed to create that "just washed" look. I raced back into the bathroom and dunked my head under the tap. I shook my hair like Max did after a bath. Then I combed the remaining water out.

There. I was ready to go.

As I raced toward the kitchen Mom stopped me at the foot of the stairs. I expected her to chew me out for the way I was dressed. Instead she put a hand on my shoulder and brushed the damp hair out of my face. She looked me up and down.

"What?" I finally said.

"It's just that . . . you're starting to look so much like your father," she said sadly.

"Mom," I said, "just because I look like him doesn't mean I'm going to turn out like him." I leaned in to kiss her on the cheek.

But she pulled away before I had the chance. "I know," she said with a faraway look in her eyes. "I know."

I suddenly realized that Don was nowhere to be seen.

Mom looked back down at me. "There's something I want to tell you," she said. "I got a phone call from Dr. Vargas today, and—"

"Where's Don?" I interrupted.

Mom paused. "He's taking a call in his study," she said.

A call! It must have come in when my head was under the tap. "No way!" I moaned.

Leaving my mother standing by the stairs, I loped down the hall toward Don's study. I entered the bookcase-lined room just as he was hanging up the phone.

From his expression I knew the whole story.

"Sorry, champ—" he started to say.

"—but you have to go into the office," I finished for him.

"You make it sound like I'm never home," he said. He placed some papers into his briefcase, not looking at me.

"Gee," I said. "Whoops. I certainly didn't mean to give you *that* impression."

Don slammed his briefcase shut.

"Look," he said defensively. "There are some things you can't understand at your age. This is one of them. But here's what we're going to do. We'll celebrate your birthday tomorrow night."

"I don't think you can do that," I said.

"Sure, I can," he said. "We're just going to put it off by one day. Okay?"

Before I could answer, he breezed past me, heading out the door.

"Like we put off camping by one day?" I asked, following him into the hall. "And the ski trip? And the car show? And the—"

"Todd!" my mother warned.

"Look," Don said, turning around to face me. "I'll make you an offer. Tomorrow we're going to do everything we were going to do tonight, and you get fifty bucks on top of it. Call it a late fine. How does that sound to you?"

"Fine," I said, fighting back tears. "Great." *That's right*, I thought. *Miss my birthday and pay me off.*

"Good," Don said with a big, phony-looking smile. "Let's get your cake started. If we hurry, I can see you blow the candles out before I have to go into the office."

"The cake!" Mom suddenly exclaimed. "I completely forgot. It's still out in the freezer."

"No big deal," I said coldly. "I'll get it."

I walked out to the garage to rescue my cake from the deep freeze, feeling my spirits plummet toward the subzero range themselves.

How could Mom forget my cake? I thought, pulling open the heavy freezer door. *How could Don be such a first-class jerk?*

At first I didn't see it through the frosty mist. A plain white bakery box, half buried beneath a bag of frozen broccoli on the bottom shelf. *Happy 13th Birthday, Todd*, read the message through the cellophane window in the lid.

It's a wonder they got my name right, I said to myself, letting the freezer door swing shut with a loud *whump*.

As I trudged back toward the kitchen Max came over and licked my hands.

At least I have one friend in this family, I thought, patting him on the head. *Even if he isn't human.*

"Fifty bucks, huh?" Bentley said later as I lay on my bed, vintage Star Wars phone receiver pressed to my ear. "A stellar outcome. Who wants to go out with their parents, anyway?"

"Yeah, I guess," I said.

"So what did you wish for?" Bentley asked.

"Oh, you know, the usual," I said. "World peace. An end to hunger. Jennifer Love Hewitt's telephone number."

I didn't want to let him know what I'd really wished for—that Mom and Don would start acting like a family.

"So how cool is that camera?" he asked.

I turned my birthday present over in my hands. It felt good to hold. It was just the right weight—solid, but not heavy. "It's an X-1000," I said. "State-of-the-art."

"I can't believe they actually got it for you," Bentley said.

"Guilt, my man," I replied. "It's the most powerful weapon any kid has."

"I wish," he said. "My parents are immune."

Your parents actually care about you, I wanted to say, *so they've got nothing to feel guilty about*. But I stopped myself. Instead I said, "So you want to check it out up close and personal?"

"Sure," he said.

"Cool." I flipped the camera strap over my neck. "I'm going to take it out to the reservoir tonight. Maybe get some admissible evidence of the existence of UFOs."

Our town, Metier, has always had a reputation as a UFO hot spot. So many people here have claimed they've seen flying saucers that folks nicknamed us the Roswell of the North. Hardly a month went by without something weird and unexplainable happening. Just last week all the video terminals and computer screens down at the mall started going haywire. The next day a trucker came into town with stories of a strange, glowing object he'd seen over the town reservoir the night before—apparently at the very same time.

It's weird. You'd think that with so many different people claiming to have seen UFOs, more people would believe in them. But just the opposite seems true. There are so many tales like this, nobody takes them seriously anymore.

Nobody but us kids, that is.

"You think that truck driver actually saw something?" Bentley asked.

I thought about what it would be like to be the first person to take a picture of an alien. It was one thing to track down a crook; it would be another to track down an extraterrestrial. I'd be famous! Even Don would have to sit up and pay attention.

"I think something's out there," I said, sounding just like Agent Mulder on the *X-Files*. "Wouldn't it be cool if we got it on film?"

"I don't know," Bentley said. "I don't know if my parents will let me go out after dark."

"What they don't know won't hurt them," I replied. "Just wait until after your parents have gone to bed and sneak out the window."

"But—I mean," Bentley stammered, "how are you going to take a picture of something at night, with no light?"

"Bentley," I said, "if a big, glowing object the size of a house landed right next to you, would *you* need a flash?"

"Okay," he said nervously, "but should we be out at the reservoir that late? It could be, you know, dangerous."

"Come on," I said. "You want to join NASA someday, right? You're going to have to go out in the dark then, won't you?"

"Yeah," Bentley said, "but I'll be wearing a space suit. With a radio. And a TV camera. And a life-support system."

"Look," I said. "If you're scared—"

"I'm not scared," he cut in. "I'm . . . apprehensive."

Finally Bentley agreed to meet me at the reservoir at midnight. I put the camera into its case, first rolling it up in a T-shirt just in case we saw any action.

I smiled to myself.

My birthday was turning out just fine, no thanks to my parents.

Chapter 3

The reservoir stank of swamp gas. I swatted the thousandth gnat out of my eyes and checked the time on my Digital Diver.

12:45 A.M. I had waited long enough.

Could I have missed Bentley? No, there were only two holes in the tall, chain-link fence that surrounded the watershed area: one by my school and the one where I was, about a quarter mile from our neighborhood. Even though the fence was posted all over with No Trespassing signs, a lot of kids still snuck in from time to time. It was supposedly cool to hang out in the woods around the reservoir.

But I sure didn't feel cool right now.

I'd been crouching in the bushes this whole

time, braving the army of mosquitoes, swamp flies, and crawling bugs that called the reservoir home. The temperature hadn't dropped much from that afternoon. The air felt like a warm, damp towel.

Sneaking out of the house had been no problem at all. Don still wasn't back at eleven, and Mom had been asleep for hours. I could have driven out in a Jeep and no one would have noticed. (Assuming, of course, that I *knew* how to drive a Jeep.)

The only problem I'd encountered was Max. He'd wanted to come, too. He whined and barked when he saw me leaving without him. I got him to quiet down by patting him on the head until he just lay watching me with his big brown eyes, his tail swishing sadly from side to side as I ducked out of the garage.

"Bentley Ellerbee," I said out loud. "I am seriously thinking about getting a new partner."

Then I pushed the jagged edges of the storm fence apart and stepped into uncharted territory.

Past the fence a dirt path cut through the trees, clearly visible in the moonlight. I followed it. After a couple of minutes the trees ended, the path dropping off sharply down a steep, rocky hill. The reservoir lay down below, stretching into the distance like a slick black mirror.

I stepped carefully onto the muddy embankment. It was harder to walk on than I thought. Before I knew it, I was on my butt, sliding out of control, desperately trying to grab onto passing bushes and tree roots.

I hit the bottom of the hill with a thud, my camera case slapping against my chest. My sport sandals were filled with a thick mixture of gravel and goo, and the seat of my jeans was so heavily coated in mud and clay that you could have baked them in a kiln. *Boy*, I thought with glee, *is Mom going to freak*.

I gingerly removed my camera from its case and checked it out piece by piece. I wouldn't know for sure whether it was okay until I tried taking some pictures, but it looked completely undamaged. So far, so good.

I looked around me. I had landed on the gravel path that ran around the body of water. The reservoir looked to be about a half mile across and perfectly round. I remembered hearing a rumour that it had been formed from the crater of a meteorite that crashed to Earth millions of years ago. I didn't doubt it.

This time of year the reservoir was almost full, its edges overgrown with cattails and reeds. The full moon sparkled over the surface of the water. Crickets chirped softly from the bushes. It was truly like being in another world.

I realized I ought to try taking some pictures to finish testing out the camera. I'd read all these stories about people who'd seen aliens but then forgot to put film in the camera or didn't take the time to focus. It would serve me right if I had a close encounter of the third kind and then the pictures didn't turn out.

I raised the camera to my eye and aimed it out over the reservoir. I steadied myself and pressed the button.

There was a tiny click and the sound of the film advancing, but no flash. No flash?

Suddenly I realized Bentley was right. What if I got the chance to take some *indoor* photography— on the alien ship!—and my flash didn't work?

I flipped the camera over, trying to read the back panel as the moon was slowly hidden behind a bank of clouds.

Why didn't I bring a flashlight? I thought, squinting in the gloom, cursing myself.

Even in the diminished light I could still make some things out. There was the place where you loaded the batteries; there was where the film cartridge went in. There was the frame counter and some heavy-duty computer stuff that I'd have to read the manual to figure out.

I couldn't believe it. This camera wasn't even a day old, way too soon to be busted! It hadn't been used or abused—except, of course, for my tumble. But still . . .

I tapped the flash with my thumb. Once, twice, three times.

Suddenly I felt a low vibration in my hands, coming from the camera. I must have set something off.

Chck!

The world was suddenly bright with spangles of blue and red. The flash had gone off in my face!

Well, I thought, blinking, *at least it's working now.*

I pointed the camera away from me.

Chck! Chck!

The flash went off again. And again.

Chck-chck-chck!

23

The camera was really humming now, like an angry wasp in my hand.

Chck-chck-chck-chck-chck-chck-chck-chck!

The flash was going off nonstop, like a strobe light. A broad swath of the reservoir was lit up in its eerie, flickering glow. It just wouldn't stop. What could be causing this? Was my camera possessed?

The whole night was suddenly filled with the same humming sound—only a million times louder. I looked up and felt the hair raise on my arms.

High above the reservoir the veil of clouds was beginning to twist together—slowly at first, but then faster and faster. They seemed lit from behind with an eerie, blue-white light.

As I watched, frozen in awe, the centre of the formation was sucked up into space. It looked like an enormous swirling funnel pointing straight up into the sky.

My heart was going a million miles a minute. I was really going to see a UFO! Or else get killed by a tornado. Either way I was ready with my camera.

I aimed my humming, glowing camera at the humming, glowing sky. My finger hovered over

24

the shutter button, ready to snap a picture the minute ET showed up.

I peered through the viewfinder. Held my breath.

There was a sudden, blinding flash of light, brighter than anything I'd ever seen before—

And everything went dark.

Chapter 4

The next thing I knew, I was in bed. What had just happened? Groggily I squirmed around, my eyes still closed, reaching for the lamp on my nightstand. I wondered what time it was. Had I just dreamed the whole business about the reservoir?

To my surprise, when I opened my eyes, the lights were already on. And to my even greater surprise, the bed I was in wasn't my own. I was in someone else's bed. Someone with much cleaner sheets.

And to my absolute and total surprise, my mom was standing over me, crying.

"He's all right," she was saying. "He's all right."

"Yes, of course he is," Don said, standing next to her in the small room. "I told you so." Don was trying to sound calm, but there was something funny about his voice. After a moment I realized what it was. He had been crying, too!

What was going on?

That was when I saw the police officers. Two of them, standing in the doorway of what I now realized was a hospital room. From the badges they wore, I could see that they were both detectives, the rank just under lieutenant. Detectives don't get involved with a case unless it's serious. They were talking in hushed tones to a grey-haired woman in a white doctor's coat.

Moments from the previous evening were starting to come back to me. Moments involving words like *trespassing* and *breaking and entering*. I knew the penalties they carried by heart.

"Mom," I said, my voice sounding surprisingly weak, "am I in a lot of trouble?"

In response my mom started kissing me on the cheeks and forehead as if I'd just come back from the dead.

"Mom, quit it," I whispered. "You're embarrassing me!"

Don smiled at the two of us. "Of course you're

not in any trouble," he said. "What makes you ask that?"

"Well . . . ," I said. I gestured to the police detectives in the corner.

"Don't worry about them," Don said. "You don't have to do anything but rest for now. You've been hurt."

"Hurt?" I asked. "What happened?"

"That's what we'd like to know," Don said.

"An hour ago you were found by the reservoir," Mom said. "You were unconscious."

Unconscious? I guess it made sense. I remembered the flash of light. "Was I struck by lightning?" I asked. I looked to see if my clothes were burned, but I was wearing one of those thin blue hospital gowns.

"Lightning?" Mom asked. She glanced nervously at the doctor, who had stepped over to my bedside. The doctor's name tag read *Strickrichter*.

"I remember a bright flash of light," I said as the doctor shone a penlight in my eyes, first the left eye, then the right. "And the clouds were all weird, like a storm was coming up. I must have passed out. Who found me?"

"Two maintenance men," Don answered. "The police are questioning them now."

"Questioning them?" I asked. "Why?"

"Because you were missing for such a long time," Mom said.

Long time? I suddenly realized I didn't know what time it was. I'd assumed it was later that night, but there were no windows in the small room. For all I knew, the sun might be shining outside. Could I have been lying outside, unconscious for hours? Maybe even a whole day? Longer?

"What day is it?" I asked.

Mom was about to answer, but Dr. Strickrichter held up a hand to silence her.

"What day do you think it is, Todd?" Dr. Strickrichter said. Her voice was soothing yet firm.

"I don't know," I said truthfully. "I guess the day after my birthday . . . Sunday, right?"

My mother gasped. Don put his arm around her shoulders, squeezing her tightly.

"Er . . . Monday?" I guessed again.

Mom turned to the doctor. "What's going on?" she cried, her voice thick with emotion. "Why doesn't he remember?"

"Please, Mrs. Aldridge," said Dr. Strickrichter. "I'm sure you're only confusing him."

I'll say, I thought.

The doctor turned to me, fixing me in her even, blue-eyed gaze. "Todd, this may come as quite a shock to you," she began. "But it's not the day after your thirteenth birthday."

"Okay," I said. My gaze flickered to the two detectives. They were staring at me expectantly. Everybody was. "So what day is it?" I continued, trying to sound clear and levelheaded.

"It's Wednesday," said Dr. Strickrichter. She cast a glance at my parents. "April twenty-second."

At first I thought I heard her wrong. "W-w-what?" I stammered.

"It's April, Todd," she repeated. "You've been missing for almost nine months."

"Are you sure you want to go home?" the doctor asked me, tucking her stethoscope into her coat pocket. "You can stay overnight if you want. We have fifty channels of cable and all the cookies you can eat."

"I think he wants to sleep in his own bed," my mother explained, stroking my hair for the thousandth time in the past half hour.

"Besides, we've got seventy-five channels at home," I muttered, and everyone laughed.

I looked around at the smiling faces and felt

like screaming, or puking, or maybe both. Why were they so happy? Did they think they could just tell me that nine whole months of my life were suddenly wiped away—poof!—and then treat it as if I'd just had a bad cold, but now was all better?

I kept on waiting for someone to yell, "April fool's!" For the doctor to pull off her mask and exclaim, "Smile, Todd, you're on *America's Wackiest Practical Jokes!*"

My eyes scanned the room hopefully, trying to see where the television camera could be hidden. Instead, I saw my stepfather lead a tall, powerfully built man into the room.

"This is Burt Rogers, chief of the Metier police department," Don said. "Do you feel well enough to answer a few questions?"

Did I? "Sure," I said.

Chief Rogers was something of a legend in our part of Wisconsin. He had been a star athlete in high school. Then like his dad, he joined the police force, working his way all the way up to the top post. His arrest record was nearly perfect. I had wanted to meet him for as long as I could remember. Some kids have Michael Jordan; I have Chief Burt Rogers.

"Great," Chief Rogers said. "So let me just ask you straight-out. Do you have any idea how you disappeared or where you've been for the past eight and a half months?"

I shook my head slowly. "I remember going to the reservoir to try to get a picture of a UFO," I said. "My camera started freaking out, and there was a bright flash of light."

"From the camera?" he asked.

"No, no, from the sky. The clouds were whirling around—"

"Yes, a storm picked up that night," he said. "So you saw some lightning?"

"I guess," I said. "I woke up here in the hospital. It seems like it just happened yesterday."

"Did someone follow you to the reservoir?" he persisted. "Did you see anyone out there, anyone at all?"

"No," I said regretfully, thinking of Bentley. If he'd shown up, at least I'd have someone to back up my story! Everyone was looking at me like I was crazy.

"What about this man?" Chief Rogers asked. He held up a close-up photograph of a thin, sinister-looking man with pasty white skin. He was grinning hideously, like the Joker. "Have you ever seen him before?"

"No," I said. But maybe I had seen him and was blanking on him, like everything else. "Not that I remember," I clarified. "Who is he?"

"We're not sure. He attacked a student at your school, Metier Junior High."

"He attacked someone? Who did he attack?" I asked.

Chief Rogers cleared his throat, seemingly embarrassed. "My son, Ethan," he said. "He's a friend of yours, isn't he?"

Friend would be stretching it. Ethan seemed like a nice guy, but I didn't really know him. It was hard to get close to him: He always had his nose in a comic book.

"Yes," I said. I held the picture, looking more closely at it. The man's eyes were glazed over with a milky white film, and his lips were discolored and blue. "He looks dead," I said.

"He is," the chief stated matter-of-factly. "This is an autopsy photo. The man died while he was trying to abduct Ethan." He glanced toward Dr. Strickrichter. "Of a . . . heart attack," he added, unconvincingly.

"Are you sure?" I asked, handing back the photo. "It looks more like poisoning to me."

The chief stared at me for a second, as if I'd

just said something I shouldn't have. I decided to change the subject. "How is Ethan doing?"

"He's fine. But we could sure use some answers. Another girl, Elena Vargas, has gone missing, and we're all very worried. We think her disappearance is somehow linked."

"Elena?" I asked. I'd had two classes with her last year. "When did she disappear?"

"Back in January," he said. "So you see it's vital that you try to come up with something, anything at all that might help us. If the same person who took you also took her, you might remember a clue that could help lead us to her."

I sat and thought. I concentrated with all my might. I sure wanted to come up with something! But no matter how hard I tried, all I could remember was that flash of light . . . and then waking up.

"I'm sorry," I said, and watched my hero's face fall in disappointment.

It's some bizarre hospital policy that all patients have to leave in a wheelchair, even if they can walk out just fine. It's pretty stupid, if you ask me. But I was so desperate to get out of that place, they could have wrapped me in a full body

35

cast and put a rainbow clown's wig on my head and I wouldn't have cared.

An hour later I was finally steered out of the hospital, Don on my left, my mother on my right. Mom was clutching my shoulder so tightly, I bet there'd be fingerprints on it the next day.

Just as we reached the car a man came out of the shadows. Fast. He was taut and muscular, like a professional athlete. In a report I would have said he was six-one and about 190 pounds, with salt-and-pepper hair. He held one hand behind his back, keeping something concealed. A gun?

I drew back. But to my surprise, the stranger's face broke into a big smile as he neared us.

"Hey!" he said. "I'm glad I caught you before you left." He looked me directly in the eyes. A large scar ran down the left side of his face, dividing his bushy black eyebrow in two. "You must be Todd," he said. "I feel like I know you already."

"You do?" I asked guardedly.

"Todd, this is Mr. Drennan," Don said. "He's a . . . friend of the family."

Whose family? I wondered. *The Addams Family?*

"These are for you," Mr. Drennan said, producing a bouquet of flowers with a flourish.

"Uh, thanks," I said, taking the bundle. I wasn't

sure if you were supposed to receive flowers as a guy.

As I was getting into the car Drennan turned to Don and whispered, "I guess my services will no longer be required."

"Money well spent," Don whispered back.

I didn't think I was supposed to hear.

Minutes later we were driving home. Mom fussed over me the whole ride. I did my best to look affectionate, but I was getting a little annoyed. I guess disappearing for nine months was what it took to get her to pay attention to me.

I suddenly realized that my birthday wish had come true—but in the weirdest possible way. I had wanted my parents to act like a loving family, and now they were.

I suppose it should have been a little comforting, to know they cared so much, but I just couldn't relax. My mind kept going back to Mr. Drennan. What was he talking about when he said his "services would no longer be required"? And was I the only one who noticed that behind his smile, his eyes were dead and cold?

We pulled into the driveway. There was everything, looking just like it did yesterday. Yesterday, that is, nine months ago.

But as I looked closer I noticed little differences. Daffodils were in full bloom along the front walk. We'd lost a tree to the winter storms. The two Frisbees I'd left on the roof were gone, the victims, I supposed, of Mom's spring cleaning.

But I didn't notice the biggest change of all until we got out of the car.

"Hey," said Don as Mom opened her door, "hang on a second, honey. I'll help you out."

Since when had Mom needed help getting out of a car? Don raced around to her side and extended a hand. "Thank you, sweetheart," she said.

I looked at the two of them, waiting for an explanation.

"Todd, do you need a hand, too?" Don asked.

"Are you kidding?" I said. "Mom, what's up here? What am I missing?"

Mom laughed softly to herself. "In all the excitement, honey, I guess I forgot to tell you." She patted her belly, which I suddenly noticed was about as large as a basketball. How could I have missed it? "Todd, you're going to have a baby sister," she announced proudly.

"A—a what?" I stammered. "When?"

"Any day now."

I stopped in my tracks, letting the news sink in. If I needed any further proof that I had been gone for nine months, here it was, staring me in the face. I suppose it was good news, but I couldn't help feeling a little creeped out. Still, a family was what I wished for when I blew out the candles on my cake, and it looked like a family was what I was getting.

"Great," I said.

Or started to say.

Because without warning, I was attacked from behind. I put out my hands as the pavement rushed up at me.

Chapter 5

"Max! Max! Max, what's wrong with you?" Don yelled as my dog stood over me, barking and snarling.

"It's okay, Don. Max just doesn't know it's me." I guess Max had learned that sneak attack trick a little too well. I reached out one hand to pet Max on the head. "That's okay, boy. It's me."

To my amazement, Max lunged for my hand, trying to bite it right off my arm!

"He must just be surprised to see me," I said, laughing. But I was uncomfortable. What was wrong with my Max?

"Honey, is that dog going to be safe for the baby?" Mom asked Don.

"It's all right! It's all right!" I said quickly. "I've

been missing so long, Max must think I'm an impostor. He's just trying to protect our house, that's all!"

"Well . . . maybe you're right," Don said, seeing the concern on my face. "Still, why don't you chain him up out back for the night?"

"Sure," I said. I reached for Max's collar, but Max crouched low, growling at me. His eyes were wild with fury. I couldn't understand it. I'd raised him from a puppy—and it was like he'd never seen me before!

"Maybe you'd better let me take him for you," Don said. He patted my dog on the head. "That's okay, Max. That's okay, boy. It's only Todd. You remember Todd."

He led the golden retriever around to the back.

We had dinner in the kitchen, just sandwiches and apple juice, but it tasted like the best food I'd ever had. Afterward I sat up until late with Mom and Don, looking at pictures of Thanksgiving and the holidays and opening still wrapped Christmas presents. It was good to see that some things hadn't changed in the last nine months. I got a new pair of in-line skates, a dozen games for my PlayStation, a mini camcorder with a built-in VCR, and my very own big screen TV.

Don's beeper went off six times while we were talking and his cell phone rang four times, but he ignored them. Finally on the fifth call he put his beeper and phone in a drawer in his study and came back to the table.

"Aren't you tired, Todd?" Mom said finally.

"No," I replied.

"Well, I'm going up to bed. I have to sleep for two now. Todd, don't stay up too late. It isn't good for you."

"He was unconscious for hours, honey," Don said. "He's liable to be wide awake for a while."

"Can I go to school tomorrow?" I asked.

Don and my mom looked at each other in surprise. "Are you sure you feel up to it?" Mom asked.

"Totally," I said. "I want to see my friends."

"I think it's a good idea," Don agreed. "Get back on the horse—that's what they taught me at business school."

"I guess so, honey, if you want," Mom said.

"I do," I replied, nodding. "Thanks, Mom."

"That's the first time I've ever heard a thirteen-year-old ask his parents' permission to go to school," Don said.

"I missed almost a whole year," I said. "I guess I've got some catching up to do."

Don turned out to be right. When I went to bed an hour later, I couldn't fall asleep. The question of where I'd been for those missing months was eating away at me. Somehow I knew there was more to it than anyone realized.

If I'd been missing that long, could I have wandered off somewhere? A scenario came to me. Maybe the flash of light had stunned me, and I'd lost my memory. I could have wandered back the way I came, to the main road, where a trucker or a passing family might have picked me up. Maybe I'd been living in another city, under another name, until now.

But if that was the case, how had I gotten back? Why hadn't I changed at all—why was my hair cut the same way, why wasn't I any fatter or thinner than the day I went down to the reservoir? And why was I unconscious when they found me?

What if someone had abducted me? Someone or . . . I remembered the unearthly hum and the glowing lights on the horizon. Someone . . . or some*thing*. What if something had been done to me? What if I were carrying a terrible disease inside me? Or what if I were carrying an *alien* inside me, an extraterrestrial stowaway that was going to burst out of my body when it was ready for its next victim? Maybe that was why Max was barking—he had smelled the creature and was frightened.

I shivered with fear in the dark. Anything could have happened. *Am I going to die?* I thought. *I'm only thirteen!*

Finally I couldn't take it any longer. I snapped on the light and got up to get a drink of water.

Mom had completely redecorated the house, probably in anticipation of my baby sister. It was going to be weird to have a sister at all, let alone one thirteen years younger than me. I drank the water standing up in the kitchen. I still didn't feel ready to go back to bed. Maybe some reading would do the trick. A big, thick book that I had trouble understanding.

Fortunately Don had left his study untouched. I found the perfect book almost immediately— the third of a four-volume set about business law. I hefted the heavy book onto my shoulder and was almost out the door when I saw the scrapbook.

It was still open on Don's desk, as if he'd left it that way when he came to see me at the hospital. I was shocked to see that every page was covered with clippings about my disappearance. How the police searched the woods with dogs. How search parties had been organized. How my picture was posted on the Internet, and on television, and on the back of milk cartons. They had even brought in psychics.

Whoa. Had it really been that big a deal?

I flipped a page. Here, Don had collected clippings about Ethan's attacker and Elena's apparent abduction, as well as a column about another classmate of mine, Ashley Rose, and how she almost drowned in the reservoir.

As I glanced over one of the many columns about me I saw a photograph of a familiar face: the salt-and-pepper hair, the bushy black eyebrows, the scar. It was Mr. Drennan, the creepy man from the hospital parking lot. Who was he really? I wondered.

The boy's parents, Mr. and Mrs. Don Aldridge, have hired private investigator Derek Drennan to look for him, the caption read. So that's what he meant by his services no longer being needed. They must have not told me who he was so that they wouldn't frighten me, I realized.

46

I carefully put the scrapbook back where I'd found it. It was nice in a way that Don cared enough to collect all those articles about me. Although part of me suspected he was doing it for tax purposes.

I crept back into bed and, with an effort of will, managed to calm myself down. But when sleep finally came, it was difficult and filled with strange, fitful dreams.

I saw myself in my favourite fantasy place: behind the wheel of a powerful police cruiser. I guess in dreams driving licenses aren't a problem.

My partner and I had just apprehended a pair of suspects. They were two teenagers with bad attitudes. We were taking them in for questioning—we had reason to believe that they were working for someone powerful.

I got a closer look at my partner. For some reason it was Ethan Rogers, Chief Rogers's son.

Ethan had that serious look on his face. I half expected to see him whip out a comic book. But he was much bigger than the Ethan I knew. His arms and neck rippled with muscle. This was not a guy to be messed with!

"What took you so long?" Ethan asked as we took the main road through town.

"What are you talking about?" I retorted. "I haven't gone anywhere. I haven't been gone at all!"

"Nine months," he replied. "I'd call that a pretty long bathroom break."

Before I could answer, the car radio squawked. "Car eleven, we have a section seven in progress. Fifth and Main."

Section seven meant a kidnapping. But we already had a full car with the two arrestees in the back. What did they want us to do?

"We're on our way," I radioed in. I flipped on the "cherries," the big flashing police lights on top of the cruiser.

"It's too much light," Bentley Ellerbee said, suddenly sitting where Ethan had been. "Much too much. The film won't come out."

I looked outside the window. He was right. The street looked like a ball of fire. Flames leaped from every building. Even the asphalt seemed to burn.

"What can we do?" I asked him.

"I don't know," Bentley said. "I guess all we can do is wait until our parents are asleep."

Then there was a flash of light. When I looked back, the car was empty. I was alone.

The police radio squawked again. "Car eleven, suspect is in range. Advise pursue on foot."

48

"Copy. Affirmative," I replied, screeching to a halt by the side of the road. I jumped out of the car and ran down the alley ahead of me.

At the end of the alley was a shadowy figure, panting, running for its life. I ran after it. It was quickly clear that I was much faster than he was. The figure tried dodging me, jumping over an overturned garbage can, but I hurdled the obstacle with ease. I was superhuman, I suddenly realized. Better than human. Faster. Stronger.

Desperately the figure tried to vault over a huge fence. But he was exhausted. He hit the edge of the fence, tripped, and fell sprawling in the center of the alley.

I approached him cautiously. He was lying face-down, apparently knocked unconscious. He was thin and bony, with black hair.

It could have been a trick, but something told me it wasn't. I put one hand on his shoulder, about to flip him over.

Then I froze.

I knew what I was going to see. This shadowy figure, the suspect I had run down . . . was me. He would have my face. Somehow I knew it.

I scratched at the back of my neck. The skin seemed loose. I could pull it off if I wanted to. I heard a dog barking in the distance.

The figure was shrinking, withering away as it lay there. I had to make a decision quickly, or the suspect was going to melt away into nothingness.

Finally, when I couldn't stand it any longer, I screwed up my courage and flipped the figure over.

It wasn't me after all. It was the pale, sinister man from the autopsy photo, his horrible blue lips pulled back in a dead man's grin.

"Nine months," he hissed, looking at me through sightless, milk white eyes. "What took you so long?"

Chapter 6

I woke to see my mother standing over me with a plate of blueberry pancakes, my favourites. "Is it time to get up already?" I asked miserably. I had hardly slept.

"The bus left about fifteen minutes ago," Mom answered, "but I can drive you this morning. Are you sure you want to go?" she asked.

"Sure, I'm sure," I said. "Just give me a few minutes to remember my own name."

Mon laughed. "I laid out your favourite suit," she said. "Just come and get me when you're ready to go."

I groaned. My favourite suit? The kids were going to laugh at me . . . and it was my first day back to school.

But I broke into a wide smile when I saw what she meant by "my favourite suit." It was my green T-shirt, jeans, and Teva sandals. She'd even managed to get them cleaned up after my mud slide. I couldn't believe this was the same mom who had once tried to get me to take ballroom-dancing lessons!

"Thanks," I said.

She winked and left the room.

I got up and stretched. Then I brushed my teeth. It was strangely comforting to be doing the same, stupid tasks I'd done every day of my life. With a toothbrush in my mouth, life felt a little more normal.

I pulled on my shirt and jumped into my pants. But as I slipped my house key around my neck, I noticed something on the nightstand by the bed.

It was my notebook, open to the very last page. There was writing on it:

Find The Others.

I looked at the words and blinked. What others? Which others? Other what? I had no idea what it meant. But something told me I should.

Because the words were in my handwriting.

*   *   *

As we pulled up in the front of Metier Junior High, Mom straightened my hair and brushed imaginary lint off my shoulders. "Mom!" I yelled, embarrassed. This being adored business had definitely gone too far.

"I just want them to see how handsome you are," she said.

"I'm not handsome, Mom," I explained, "I'm thirteen."

She kissed me good-bye and I stepped out of the car, grabbing my backpack as I went.

I guess I should have realized from Don's scrapbook that my disappearance was pretty big news. What I didn't count on was what big news my reappearance would be. The entrance to the school was mobbed with reporters from every major paper—including Martin Treadweather from Channel Three News and his entire camera crew. As soon as he saw me, he motioned to his cameraman. Soon I was blinded by lights and flashbulbs.

"How does it feel to be back, Todd?" Treadweather called out, his fake white teeth flashing.

"Where have you been for the last nine months?" asked a woman with a tape recorder.

Then they all started shouting at once.

"Have you seen Elena Vargas?"

"Were you abducted by aliens?"

"Can you tell us who kidnapped you?"

"Was it all just a prank?"

Suddenly a hand grabbed my shoulder. I looked up, to see that Mr. Lower, the school headmaster, had appeared at my side. "Excuse me. Excuse me!" he shouted at the reporters, pushing his glasses up on his nose. "This is a school. Todd is one of our students and a minor. You people should know better than this. Todd has made his statement to the police. Now, if you'll excuse us, he's going to go back to being a seventh-grader."

Placing his hand on my shoulder, Principal Lower led me through the double doors into the building. We walked down the hallway toward my new class room. It all seemed so familiar, yet so strangely different. The walls were covered with a mural that I'd never seen before. I recognized the names of some of my friends along the base of it.

"Mrs. Ledbetter, this is Todd Aldridge," Principal Lower said when we reached the classroom. "He's going to be in your form for the rest of the year."

"We're glad to have you, Todd," said Mrs. Ledbetter, a pretty young woman in a light sweater and khakis. She smiled at me.

Then I turned to face the rest of the class.

Twenty-four stunned students looked back at me. It felt as if the whole room was holding its breath. Like I had some germs they didn't want to catch. *This is going to be tough*, I thought.

After the form time bell rang, I headed out into the hallway. Someone tapped me on the shoulder.

"Hey, Todd," said the excited voice behind me. "I can hardly believe you're back!"

I turned around. I almost did a double take. It was Bentley Ellerbee. But he was taller than I was!

"I was going to come by last night," he continued, "but my mom said you probably needed your sleep."

I couldn't stop staring at him.

"What?" he asked. "If you're mad about that night, I swear I tried to go. But my mom was up late, and—"

"I'm not mad," I said. "I'm not mad. I just can't believe it's you. Look at you! You grew, what, nine inches!"

"Yeah," he said, showing a big, gapped-tooth smile. "Ten, actually. I hardly notice it unless I'm buying clothing."

"Well, you said you were going to hit a growth spurt," I said, smiling.

"Hey, do you have a schedule yet?" he asked.

"No, why?" I asked.

"Because maybe you can hang with me for the day. I've got Mr. Blanchard next. He's pretty cool. We're reading *Dr. Jekyll and Mr. Hyde* right now. You know, the one about the mad scientist?"

I smiled, thinking, *Of course Bentley likes it—it's about a scientist*. "Uh, sure, right," I said. I suddenly realized that this was how it was going to be in every class: I was behind everywhere. Why had I ever wanted to come back to school in the first place? With the massive amount of catching up I had to do, they'd probably make me repeat the seventh grade!

"*Dr. Jekyll and Mr. Hyde*," the tall blonde man at the front of the class said. He looked kind of like Brad Pitt but with long hair and a beard. "The story of a scientist who develops a drug that splits him

56

into two competing personalities. Half the time he's a perfectly nice guy. The other half he's a monster."

Mr. Blanchard had dressed up in a cape and top hat for the class. He put on a two-sided mask. One half was human, and the other half looked like Don on a bad day.

"You can read this book like a simple horror story, and it's pretty good," he said through the mask. "Or if you're smart, you'll look deeper. What's this guy really trying to say? He's saying that in each one of us, there's a monster . . . if we let it out."

He took off the mask. "Does anyone remember where we are?"

"Dr. Jekyll just woke up from a dream to find strange writing on his books," Toni Douglas said. "And then he realizes that the handwriting is his own."

"Good," Mr. Blanchard said. "And what problem does our hero face now?" he asked.

"He has to get rid of the monster without destroying himself," Bentley said.

"An excellent summary," Mr. Blanchard said. "Now, let us read."

Mr. Blanchard flipped open his book and started reading aloud. The story seemed interesting, if you'd started from the beginning. But I was completely lost. I followed along for a little while, but then gave up. For some reason, I couldn't concentrate. I was beginning to hear a strange, low buzzing sound. Where was it coming from?

I glanced out the window. It was a pretty warm day for April. The caretaker, Mr. Dailey, was cutting the lawn outside. His bald head gleamed in the sunlight. The smell of freshly cut grass floated in as Mr. Blanchard read on and on. Could I be hearing Mr. Dailey's lawn mower? I wondered.

I looked back down at my book, thinking I'd drift off for a few minutes. The letters on the page started to swim, the way they do when your eyes cross. And the buzzing was getting louder. Now it sounded almost like a dog's growl.

I thought about Max. What was wrong with him? I decided I'd try to feel him out when my parents weren't around, after I got home. I knew the situation was serious. If Mom thought Max would be dangerous for the new baby, there was no way I could save him.

It was funny how the letters were crossing.

They seemed to spell out new words. Suddenly I realized that they had arranged themselves into a new sentence. The letters stood out starkly from the blur of the other words on the page, so black that they seemed to suck the light right out of the room.

FIND THE OTHERS. DO NOT FAIL.

_____ **Chapter 7**

I was so surprised that I almost stood up. I managed to get control of myself. I looked around. No one had seen anything but me.

I looked back down at the book. Of course, it had gone back to normal.

Maybe, I told myself, it was one of those "Magic Eye" books, where if you stare at it the right way a 3-D image pops up. But I knew that couldn't be it. Magic Eye books are made with special computers, and Robert Louis Stevenson died way before computers were invented.

I looked over at Bentley. He was following along with Mr. Blanchard's reading, tapping a pencil on his thigh. The janitor was still cutting the grass outside. In the second row from the front Lynette Barbini passed a note to Toni Douglas. It was a regular classroom.

Find the others. Do not fail.

What was wrong with me?

Finally the bell rang.

At least, I thought, *nothing weird can happen at lunch.*

"Aaaagh!" yelled Nick Carlucci as I sat down at the cafeteria table. "It's got me! The alien's got me!"

He slowly sank under the table, thrashing and grabbing at the "alien"—a soup thermos with a pair of glasses attached to the lid.

"Shut up, simp," said Vinnie Carlucci, punching Nick on the leg. "The guy's been, like, abducted."

Nick and Vinnie were identical twins who hated each other's guts. I had never heard them agree on anything in the eight years I'd known them. Sometimes they'd get into a fistfight and a teacher would have to grab one of them by the shirt and pull them apart, looking for all the world like she was standing in front of a mirror. Nick and Vinnie hated each other so much that you would have thought they'd keep far away from each other, but for some strange reason they went everywhere together. They dressed alike, got the same haircuts, went to the same movies—and spilled popcorn all over the seats arguing about whether or not the movie stunk.

"Who are you calling a simp?" Nick wanted to know.

"Cut it out, guys," Bentley said. "So, Todd, are you having a good first day back?"

"Sure," I said, hoping my friends didn't see that I was still shaking from what I'd seen in English class.

"What did you think of Mr. Blanchard's costume? Pretty over the top, huh?" Bentley asked.

"Oh, come on," said Willy McIntyre, the only redhead in our group. "Let's ask Todd what we really want to ask him. You don't mind, do you, Todd?"

"No," I said, "but I don't really remember anything."

"Okay," said Nick. "I'll go first." He looked at me. "Todd, would you call my brother Vinnie mentally challenged or mentally stunted?"

"Shut up!" said Vinnie, punching Nick on the arm.

"I think it could have been a wormhole," said Bentley.

"A what?" I asked.

"A tunnel between our universe and another one. You said you saw, like, a funnel and a flash of light, right?"

"Yeah," I said.

"That sounds like it," Bentley said. "*Voomp*, the wormhole opens up. A big tunnel in the sky, right over the reservoir. It sucks you up. You spend an instant in the other universe, but on Earth it's nine months. Then bam, it spits you back out. That's when the maintenance workers found you."

"That's how it felt, like only an instant had gone by," I said slowly. "It felt like no time passed at all. One second I was looking up, and the next I was lying in the hospital."

"Why wasn't he killed by the fall?" Nick asked.

"Maybe the wormhole touched down, like a tornado touches down," Bentley said.

"Why did it only get Todd?" Willy asked. "Why wasn't the whole reservoir missing?"

"Maybe it only picks up life-forms," Bentley said.

"Okay," said Vinnie, "but what about the other

life-forms there? Like the bugs and stuff? Why didn't it get those, too?"

"Maybe it did," Bentley said. "Would you notice if a few bugs were missing from the reservoir for nine months?"

"Yeah," I said, "the police don't exactly put their pictures on milk cartons. But why would it do that? Why would a wormhole just—*open up?*"

Bentley looked at me for a long moment. "I have no idea," he said finally. "I don't think anybody does."

I looked up to see a girl with long brown hair walking through the cafeteria toward me. She was dressed in black jeans, black combat boots, and a black T-shirt, with a huge black knapsack slung over her shoulder. Ashley Rose.

"Don't look now," Willy whispered to me, "but here comes Splashley Rose."

"Why are you calling her Splashley?" I wanted to know, but by then she was within hearing range.

"I have one more question, Professor," Vinnie was saying.

"Yes?" Bentley asked.

"Why do you think Nick smells so bad all the time?"

65

"That's it," Nick said, dumping Vinnie's milk carton into his lap.

"Todd?" Ashley said, standing behind me. "There's someone on the phone for you. Can you come with me?"

If I hadn't been so caught up by Bentley's theory, I probably would have asked Ashley who the phone call was from, or why they sent her to get me. I barely knew Ashley Rose—we'd never had classes together, and we weren't exactly friends. But that didn't stop me from following her out of the cafeteria.

Practically everybody at the school was either eating lunch or in class. Technically you were supposed to have a pass just to be in the hallway, or you'd get written up. The hallway was deserted. Deserted, that is, except for Jack Raynes.

I groaned as I realized I'd walked into yet another trap by our class prankster. "What is it, Jack?" I asked. "Do you want to insult me for what I'm wearing? Or do you think it's funny that I've been missing for nine months?"

But the minute I'd said the words, I realized that something strange was going on. This wasn't the same Jack that had tormented me all through grade school. This wasn't the same Jack that tried to trip me at the mall.

This Jack was serious.

"No, I don't think it's funny," he said. "I don't think it's funny at all."

Just then Ethan Rogers came running around the corner. At first he looked the same as I remembered—small and kind of nerdy. You'd never guess he was Chief Rogers's son. But while he used to be awkward and shy, now he looked quick and powerful. He had a strange confidence behind his eyes.

"It's clear," Ethan said. Then he noticed me. "Hi, Todd," he said. "How are you feeling?"

He was the first person outside of my family to say that and sound genuinely concerned. What was a guy like Ethan doing with Jack? And what were both of them doing with Ashley Rose?

"I'm fine," I said. "What's going on? What's with bringing me out here?"

Ethan took a step closer. "Todd, my dad said that you don't remember anything about the time you spent missing. Is that true? Or is that just what you have to tell people?"

"No, it's true," I said. "I feel like I was never gone at all. Bentley thinks I may have gone into a wormhole." I wasn't sure if they'd know what that meant, but it seemed to mean something to Ethan.

Ashley let out a sigh of disappointment. "Todd," she said, "there's something going on in our town. Something big. Something that makes *Independence Day* look like *Bambi*."

I was getting a funny feeling, looking at the three of them together. My ears started to tingle. The words came back to me.

Find the others. Do not fail.

My gaze scanned the three faces in front of me. I was reminded of Don's scrapbook. There had been clippings on Ethan and Ashley. Had something bad happened to Jack as well?

"You guys were friends of Elena Vargas, right?" I asked, doing my best impression of a police interrogation. "Is that what this is all about?"

"We're more than *friends* of Elena Vargas," Ashley said softly. "And you may not know it yet, but you are, too."

"What are you talking about?" I asked. The tingling was becoming a buzzing sensation.

"Todd, your father disappeared nine years ago, right?" Jack asked. "On July fifth?"

"Yes," I said, surprised to hear that date. I

thought only my mother and me knew. "So?"

"So," he said, "my father did too. So did Ashley's mother. And Elena's father. And Ethan's real parents—the chief adopted him."

"What are you saying," I asked, "that they all went somewhere together? Vacation in the Bahamas? A big fishing trip?"

"Maybe they went somewhere," Jack replied, "but I don't think it was fishing."

"Todd, have you had any strange sensations recently?" Ethan asked. "Any unexplainable headaches or dizziness?"

"No," I said, trying to ignore the buzzing that was growing louder by the second.

"What about special skills?" Ashley said.

"Skills?" I repeated. "Like what?"

"I can fight like a trained warrior," Ethan said. "Ashley can breathe underwater. Jack can understand any language. Elena was psychic. All of these abilities started to show themselves on our thirteenth birthdays. Do you see what I'm getting at?"

"Sure," I said slowly. "You're saying that your parents were aliens, and that you have mutant powers, and that you're leading secret identities."

"Exactly," Ethan said.

"Except you forgot one thing," I said.

"What's that?" Ethan asked.

"You're nuts," I said. "You've been reading too many comic books."

Ethan threw his hands up in the air. "You've been missing for nine months! You saw something big in the sky and a flash of light! Where do you think you went?"

"Someone kidnapped me—" I started.

"Someone kidnapped you without asking for a ransom? They fed you, gave you clothes and a bed for nine months, and then you wake up . . . by the reservoir?"

"Look," I said, "I can understand forgetting something I learned in class. I can understand forgetting the combination to my locker. But if I had been abducted by space aliens and spent nine months on a UFO, I think I'd remember it." The buzzing in my head was now a dull throbbing.

"We saw Elena get taken up by a UFO," Ethan said. "We saw it with our own eyes."

"And you think it was her alien father who took her?" I scoffed. "That our missing alien parents are trying to take us back to their home planet? Come on!"

"Not our parents," Ashley said solemnly. She peered into my eyes. "Our parents' *enemies*."

I must have looked as confused as I felt.

"It's like this," Jack said. "We know our parents disappeared, all on the same day. Why? We think it's because they were hiding here on earth, but then they were found out."

"By their enemies," Ashley cut in.

Jack nodded. "Maybe they were caught, maybe they escaped, but whatever happened, they had to leave us behind."

"Perhaps they thought we'd be safe here," Ethan said, "that they'd managed to keep our identities hidden. After all, we kids looked perfectly human, and acted perfectly human . . . up until our thirteenth birthdays."

"Because that's when our powers manifested themselves," said Ashley.

"And that's when the alien assassins showed up," Jack added with a shudder.

"Alien assassins?" I blurted. "Do you know how nutso this all sounds?"

"We're dead serious," Ethan said. "Each of us has fought with a shape-shifting alien freak around our thirteenth birthday. We three managed to escape. Elena Vargas wasn't so lucky."

"And what about me?" I demanded. "If an alien assassin abducted me on my birthday, what am I doing back? Why didn't it kill me?"

"That's what *we'd* like to know," Jack replied.

"And that's why we want you to join us," Ethan added. "So that we can figure this out together."

"Well, I've already figured out something on my own," I said. "The three of you are out of your minds."

"He needs proof," Ashley said. She slung her backpack off her shoulder.

Jack winced. "I thought we weren't going to do this anymore," he said.

Ashley removed a safety pin from her backpack. "Prick yourself," she said, holding it toward me. "You'll see. Your blood is silver. Silver like ours."

"Come on," I said, "don't do this. Don't you think this has gone far enough?" I could barely hear over the painful throbbing in my head, anyway. With every massive pulse, the words were practically standing out in front of me:

FIND THE OTHERS. DO NOT FAIL.

I could almost reach out and touch them.

Jack passed me the pin. "Do it," he said. "It convinced me."

72

I looked at the pin in my hands. It was crazy, but at least it would get rid of them. I needed to go somewhere quiet and think. I needed to escape the buzzing pain.

"Fine," I said, and put the pin against my thumb.

Just then loud footsteps came around the corner. "Do I hear voices?" came a woman's harsh voice.

"Mrs. Martinez," Ethan said. "Quick, let's get out of here!"

Ethan and Jack dashed down the hallway. Ashley ducked into the girls' room. I was left standing alone by the phones, holding a large pin behind my back. *Great*, I thought, *this doesn't look too suspicious.*

Mrs. Martinez rounded the corner. She was a heavyset woman with thick black hair that she kept in a bun on top of her head. One look at her was compelling evidence that not all of us had descended from apes: Some of us had cows in our family trees.

"Young man?" she asked, glaring down at me severely through her thick black glasses. "What are you doing in the hall? Do you have a pass?"

"No," I said. "I'm . . ." I had to think quickly.

73

"I'm waiting for my mom. I don't feel so well, so I'm asking my mom to take me home early."

She looked skeptical.

"I've been missing for nine months, you know," I said.

"You're Todd Aldridge?" she asked. I nodded. "You poor dear," said Mrs. Martinez, her face suddenly becoming softer. "Wouldn't you rather wait in the nurse's office?" she asked.

"No, thank you, Mrs. Martinez," I said. "I'll wait right here."

I suddenly became aware of a damp sticky sensation in my hand. In my surprise I'd accidentally pricked my thumb! And I was still holding the pin behind my back.

"Well, I'd better just wait here with you," she said, "in case you feel faint."

In fact, I was feeling faint at that very moment. How much blood had I lost? It felt like a quart. That thing had been sharp! What were they trying to do, kill me?

"That's all right," I told Mrs. Martinez. "It could be a long time before she gets here."

"It's no trouble," she said. "I don't have another class until seventh period."

Great. How long could I stand here like this,

bleeding? It was my first day back, and I was going to be suspended. It would take a miracle to get me out of this one.

Suddenly the doors at the end of the hall opened. A woman came in from the parking lot. I saw, to my utter disbelief, that it was my mother!

"They said they were going to call you to the front office," Mom said, looking confused.

A good cop can think on his feet. "I must have gotten it mixed up," I said. "I'm feeling a little disoriented."

"I'm Mrs. Martinez," the teacher said. "I teach Spanish."

"Carol Aldridge," Mom said quickly. "I'm sorry, we're in a hurry. Todd, are you ready to go?" she asked me. "Where are your books?"

"In my locker," I said. "I don't need them."

"Let's go, then," she said.

As we walked rapidly toward the car I snuck a peek at my thumb.

The blood welling up from the cut was a dull, unmistakable silver.

Chapter 8

"Did they tell you what's going on?" Mom wanted to know as we sped toward Metier's downtown.

"No," I said truthfully.

"Chief Rogers found a psychiatrist who specializes in hypnotism. He thinks the psychiatrist can help you remember where you were when you were missing. He doesn't want to waste any time."

She looked at me, worried. "Do you feel up to this, Todd?" she asked.

The truth was that I didn't, and for lots of reasons. For one thing, what if while I was in a hypnotic trance I blurted something about my silver blood? I might wake up in some secret government lab with a bunch of *X-Files* guys doing experiments on me, probing my brain with long needles. For another reason, the very idea of going back to those nine missing months terrified me. I wasn't sure what they'd find out when they hypnotized me. Maybe nothing. But I had a feeling that there was something to uncover—and that it was scary and evil.

Still, there was a girl missing. Elena. I thought about how worried her parents must be. I didn't believe Ethan's crazy story about seeing her abducted by a UFO—no matter what colour my blood was. She could be in terrible danger at that very instant. It didn't matter how scared I was. I had to try to help. It was my duty.

"Sure," I said. "This should be fun."

The words sounded a lot more certain than I felt.

Mom dropped me off in front of a large, three-story brick mansion. She had to visit her doctor, but promised to pick me up in a couple hours. As her dark blue Volvo pulled away, I got a closer look at the old building. It looked like something out of a Stephen King novel. Dark curtains were drawn in all the windows, and the whole house was covered with ivy.

I walked up the crumbling slate path to the front steps. I sure hoped this guy was a better doctor than he was a gardener. The front lawn was dead and full of weeds.

There was a tarnished brass plaque next to the front door.

MORTIMER STRANG, M.D.

I raised my fist and was about to knock on the door when it was swiftly pulled open. "Come in, young boy," said a tall, old man with long white hair brought back in a ponytail and piercing, dark brown eyes. "You must be Todd." Before I could respond, he motioned me inside. The door slammed behind us with a loud bang.

I was led through a dimly lit corridor and into what I guessed was the old man's office.

The room was dark and musty: The shades were drawn tightly, and there was the smell of old leather in the air. Sunlight peeked in from around the shades, capturing motes of dust in the air like a spray of falling stars.

I could barely see at first, but my eyes gradually

made out an enormous carved-wood desk and an equally outsized couch made from dark leather. A row of small brass mechanisms glinted dimly on a ledge over the fireplace. I walked toward them, trying to figure out what they were.

"Stop right there!" Dr. Strang exclaimed, and I jumped about a foot in the air.

He chuckled. "What I mean to say is, we should get to know each other before you enter the sanctum sanctorum," he continued, "the place where I do my most private work. My name is Dr. Strang."

"I know," I said. "They told me." *Add an* e *to the end*, I thought, *and you'd hit it on the head*.

"Do you feel comfortable? Or a little nervous? It's important that I know."

"I'm a little worried," I said, "but just because I've never done this before. It's nothing I can't handle."

"Of course not," he said, nodding. "Hypnotism is nothing to be nervous about. In Latin it simply means 'sleep.' When I hypnotize you, I bring you into a deep state of relaxation, where your inner mind—what we call the unconscious—will be able to speak its piece. There's nothing magical about it."

That didn't sound so bad. The fact was, I could use some sleep after the dreams of the previous night. But somehow his speech wasn't helping.

"It will be completely up to you, Todd," he continued. "If you don't want to be hypnotized, you can't be hypnotized. It's a simple fact."

I took a deep breath. I didn't really want to be hypnotized—but I was going to have to get over that. Elena's life might depend on it.

"Okay," I said, "I'm ready."

He chuckled again. "Look at you, standing there like that," he said. "You look like we're going to have a boxing match. Why don't you lie down on the couch and get comfortable? Nothing's going to happen here that you don't want to happen."

"Right," I said, "okay." I guess I was being a little defensive. But I couldn't help it! I lay down on the couch and settled in. The leather was warm and reassuring.

Dr. Strang opened a small closet and took out a video camera and a tripod. It was the same kind I had just received for Christmas. He screwed the camera into the tripod. "Does this bother you?" he asked. "The police want me to make a tape of our little session in case there's something that might be admissible in court."

"No," I said. "That's fine." The idea that I was doing this as part of the ongoing investigation gave me courage. I had to get through this—or Chief Rogers himself would see me fail on videotape.

Dr. Strang placed a mini cassette in the camera, then turned the camera on with a sharp click. The tape whirring through the reels sounded very loud in the small room. "I saw you looking at my collection when you came in," he said, pointing at the row of brass objects. "Can you see them from where you're lying?"

"Yes," I said.

"Do you know what they are?" he asked.

"No," I said. I was starting to feel a little drowsy.

"They're instruments that sailors used to find their way when they were out at sea. You know, they didn't have any phones or radios back then. If you were lost in the middle of the ocean, hundreds of miles from land, it must have been a very frightening thing." He crossed over to the sill. "Do you want to know their names?" he asked.

I nodded.

"This one is called a sextant," he said, touching what looked like a short telescope attached to a sundial. "This one is an astrolabe. And this one is also an astrolabe, but a special kind the Dutch used for their most dangerous voyages. It's called a captain's astrolabe."

He picked up the most complex instrument on the shelf, a series of golden pendulums in a glass box. "And this is my prize," he said. "A marine chronometer, used to tell the time when you couldn't make out the sun because the sky was cloudy or it was night. This belonged to Captain James Cook, the greatest navigator of the eighteenth century."

He set the small balls inside the chronometer rocking from side to side. I followed their motion with my eyes. I felt myself slipping under. *No!* something screamed inside me. *I mustn't!* I fought down my panic, concentrating on the doctor's words.

"You're lost at sea yourself, aren't you, Todd?" he asked. "You don't know where you've come from. You don't know where you've been. And where you are . . . is uncertain."

The terror I was feeling was just a low buzz underneath my thoughts. I struggled to lie calm.

Again I felt myself slipping far, far away. . . .

"I want to take you back there, Todd," the doctor said. "I'm going to take you back."

No, the small voice inside me said feebly. *Can't go . . . back. Mustn't go—*

And then, just like that, it was silent.

Chapter 9

When I came to, my heart was racing like it might burst. I was frightened out of my mind. I was huddled in a tight ball, my muscles tense, ready to spring if I were found out.

For some reason everything smelled of bleach.

He's after me! my thoughts screamed. *Must stay hidden!*

I was panic-stricken, trying to piece together what had just happened. Once again my memory was of no use. There was a dark stretch that I couldn't penetrate.

Cautiously I opened my eyes. It was still dark. I could see a faint sliver of light. Slowly I realized that I was in a closet. For some reason that rang a bell. I vaguely had the sense that I'd locked myself in.

I struggled bitterly, but that was all that came back. All I knew was that whatever had happened, I had barely escaped with my life. And whatever I had escaped from might still be out there.

Then I heard footsteps.

I groped around in the dark, trying to find anything that might help me. There was a mop handle, a dustpan with a broom, a can that I thought might be Comet. Could I throw it in my attacker's face? What would a detective do?

Suddenly the door was thrown open. The light was blinding. I found myself looking directly into the face of . . . Chief Rogers!

"The boy's all right!" he yelled to some of his men behind him. "He's over here!"

He offered me a hand. "Here, son," he said. "Let's get you out of there."

I had never been so glad to see another person in my life. I took his hand and stood. My clothes felt funny. I looked down, to see that my T-shirt was ripped down the neck, my jeans were torn. All around me people stopped and stared, shopping bags in their hands.

Wait a second. Shopping bags? I looked around at the familiar sights: the escalators, the glass storefronts, the little cart where they sold ceramic mugs.

I was in the mall! We were at least ten miles from Dr. Strang's office! I looked at Chief Rogers. "Wha-what happened?" I stammered. My heart was only starting to calm down now.

"Don't you worry about that just yet," he said. "There'll be time enough to explain once we get you back to your own home."

On the ride to my house the chief explained what little the police knew about what had happened. "As far as we can tell," he said, "someone broke into the doctor's office in the middle of your session. He assaulted the doctor and tore the place apart. The office is utterly demolished. It looks like a small army went through there."

I thought about the row of delicate sailor's instruments on Dr. Strang's shelf. They had probably been destroyed. "What does Strang say happened?" I asked.

"Dr. Strang can't say much, I'm afraid," Chief Rogers replied. "He was hurt pretty badly. He's lucky to be alive. What about you? Do you remember anything?"

"No," I said, feeling like the least competent

junior police officer in the world. "My mind is a blank. It's funny that I didn't wake up during the attack."

"Not really," he said. "You were under hypnosis, after all."

I snapped my fingers. "Wait a second! He was videotaping the session! Have you checked the camera?"

"Yeah, we thought of that," the chief said, turning onto my street. "The tape is the only thing missing from the office. We did have one stroke of luck, though. The doctor's next-door neighbour saw a tall, pale-skinned man leaving the office, then driving the doctor's car into town. We found the car abandoned outside the shopping mall. That's how we found you."

A tall, pale-skinned man? I suddenly had a thought. "Maybe he's related to the guy who attacked Ethan," I said, "the one in the autopsy photo."

"That's what I think, too," the chief said. He pulled into my driveway. "We suspect that he was trying to abduct you and we scared him away," he concluded.

"But what about motive?" I asked. "Why would he bother doing all of this?"

The chief looked down at his hands. "It only adds up to one thing," he said. "Someone doesn't want you remembering what happened during those nine months."

The house was dark and the door was locked, but I told the chief I'd be okay. I knew I needed to be alone. I had to figure out what was going on.

What Ethan and the others had said to me—had I ruled that out too quickly? My blood was silver, like they said it would be. But I didn't have any superpowers. And there hadn't been any alien assassins. Unless . . .

Could it be? Could it have been an alien who attacked Dr. Strang and kidnapped me? It sounded crazy. But so did not being able to explain where I'd been for nine months. If it had been an assassin, why hadn't it killed me on the spot? Why take me to the mall? Was there a ship waiting near there—a ship that would take me to where Elena had gone?

So far, all I had were questions. I needed some facts. I decided to call someone who knew something about this: Ethan Rogers.

I walked into the mudroom, senses on full

alert. It was my own house, but after the day I'd had, everything seemed sinister. Where was Mom? She should have been home from the doctor by now. Max was barking furiously out back. Poor Max. The sooner I figured out what was going on, the sooner we could be pals again.

I edged around the corner into the kitchen, my back against the wall SWAT-team style. I sure hoped they weren't preparing a nine-month-late surprise party. I could just see turning the corner to find everyone waiting for me, yelling, "Surprise!" I'd look like an idiot.

But no one was there. The ticking of the wall clock sounded unnaturally loud, as did my heartbeat. Where was everybody?

That's when I saw the note on the oven. I edged closer. *Todd*, the note read in Don's big, block-letter handwriting. *We're at the hospital! You're about to have a baby sister!*

My mind reeled. I couldn't believe it! Today of all days! Of course I was happy, but . . .

Some part of me realized that I had other responsibilities. The birth of my baby sister would be one of the most special events in my parents' lives. But I had a job to finish, and it had to come first. Otherwise I could be bringing the danger that was after me into my own home.

I picked up the phone and dialed. "Hello," I said when Mrs. Rogers answered. "Is Ethan there?"

They must have been eating dinner. I thought I detected the sound of silverware being laid down, a kitchen chair scraping across the floor.

"Hellwro?" said a boy's voice, over a mouthful of food.

"Ethan," I said, surprised to hear myself talking in a whisper. "You guys were right. It came after me."

"Todd?" Ethan said, swallowing. "Is that you? What happened?" As he was talking, the strange buzzing began again in my head. I began to feel dizzy and nauseated. I clutched my forehead.

"Todd?" Ethan continued. "Are you still there?"

"I'm here," I said, trying to ignore the pain. "And I believe you."

"Where are you? Are you safe?"

"I'm home," I replied. "I think I'm safe for now."

"Good," Ethan said. His voice grew lower.

91

"Listen, Todd. It's not a good idea to talk like this. We should get together."

"Let's rendezvous tonight," I said automatically, "at the reservoir." The words didn't seem my own. It felt like I was reading out loud in class, from a book someone else had written. "All of us."

"Great," Ethan said. "I'll call the others. When?" he asked.

"At midnight," I said, my lips moving entirely on their own. I said good-bye, then hung up.

I looked at the clock. It was nearly eight. I had four hours. Should I try to get a ride to the hospital? I wondered. I realized it was out of the question. Once I got there, my parents probably wouldn't let me out of their sight. I needed to see Ethan, Ashley, and Jack that night. Something told me that my life might depend on it.

Instead I thought I'd go upstairs and call Bentley. Maybe he'd have some more information. But as I hurried up the stairs I felt something cold and hard in my jeans pocket. What could it be? I hadn't taken anything to school heavier than my calculator—and that was in my locker.

I reached into my pocket and pulled out the hard, square lump. When I saw what it was, I almost fainted from shock.

_____ Chapter 10

The object in my hand was a mini videocassette. It was clearly labelled in red pen:

Subject: Todd Aldridge
Examiner: Mortimer Strang
Date: 4/23

It was the tape missing from Dr. Strang's office. I had taken it. But why? Several possibilities came to mind. All of them made my blood run cold.

I ran down to the rec room, tape in hand. I didn't want to see what was on it, but I knew that I had to. I switched the TV on, popped the tape in my new VCR, and pressed play.

The picture quality was poor—there wasn't enough light. But there was the doctor's office, just as I remembered it. I could definitely make out Dr. Strang, with his weird ponytail. And there I was, lying on the couch. My face was slack and my eyes were closed as if I were sleeping, but every muscle in my body was tight.

"I'm going to take you back," the doctor was whispering. "Just stretch out with your mind. Think. Come with me. It's a warm August night. You're all alone at the reservoir. What do you see?" he asked.

"The clouds . . . they're moving," I answered. It was weird watching myself on tape, saying words I didn't remember saying.

"And then what happened?" Strang asked.

"And then . . ." My voice trailed off. Something strange was happening to the picture. My face was oddly distorted.

"Yes?" Strang prompted.

"And then . . . ," I said. My entire face was twitching and moving around, as if there was something alive inside my skin. The doctor leaned in, a look of concern on his face.

"Todd?" he asked. "Todd, are you okay? Can you hear me?"

I thrashed back and forth, spasming, as if I'd been shot with a Taser gun. I hunched into a tight ball, my face buried in the leather of the couch.

The doctor bent over me. "Todd?" he asked. "Todd, snap out of it!" He put a hand on my shoulder and shook me.

On the video I turned over and faced the doctor. I stared straight at him.

Strang backed up a few steps, terrified. He opened his mouth, but no words came out.

You could see my face clearly. My eyelids were open. But the sockets were empty. No, not quite empty—where my eyes should have been were black, soulless disks, twin voids that seemed to suck the air right out of the room.

I was an assassin.

An *alien* assassin.

I realized that I had been all along.

"Todd?" the creature on the tape hissed. "I'm afraid Todd isn't in right now."

My arms and legs began to stretch. My skin became waxy and pale. My hair thinned, looking like an older man's. I had been waiting a long time for my body to change, but this was going a little too far.

The doctor tried desperately to backpedal, but in his haste he tripped and fell over backward.

"I'm sorry," the alien hissed. "Your time is up."

In a single, swift motion the assassin leaped from the couch and pounced, its teeth bared. There was the sound of a frantic struggle. Mercifully I didn't see any of it—it all happened out of frame.

There was a final scream, and then everything went silent.

When it had finished, the creature stood up and looked directly into the camera. "If you're watching this, Todd," the creature hissed, "you have already completed the necessary part of your mission."

It was talking to me! How did it know I'd be watching the tape? And what mission was it talking about?

"You see," the monster continued, "if you haven't already figured it out by now, you're not Todd at all. You're me."

To actually see myself transformed—then to actually hear it from the voice of this eyeless monster—was a shock I was unprepared for. But I couldn't deny it:

I was an alien. And an ugly alien at that.

But then why do I think I'm Todd Aldridge?

As if in response, the creature on the tape continued. "You, or should I say, *I,*" the creature hissed, "had to impersonate Todd Aldridge in order to win the others' complete trust. I was even implanted with Todd Aldridge's memories to make the disguise foolproof."

So that was the answer. Not only did they make me look like Todd, they had given me his past. Somehow they injected my brain with his memories, just like downloading a computer disk.

It was the ultimate mind warp! What I had just seen seemed beyond belief—but I knew it had to be the answer. There was no other way to explain my experiences of the last few days. Sherlock Holmes had a saying: When you eliminate the impossible, whatever remains, no matter how crazy, must be the truth. Well, I was staring the truth in the face, and I still couldn't believe it.

I was one of the shape-shifting assassins that my friends had warned me about. And as it turned out, I wasn't the one in danger—*they were in danger from me!* Of course they had fallen for it. Heck, even *I* was convinced I was Todd

Aldridge. Apparently Max was the only one who hadn't been fooled.

"You may think you're Todd now," the assassin said, "but soon your real identity will take back over. Don't fight it. Tonight at midnight we will rendezvous with the mother ship. Victory is ours!"

Wait a minute. Midnight. Rendezvous. Where had I heard those words before?

Suddenly I realized. I had asked Ethan to meet me at the reservoir at midnight. I was leading him and the others straight into a trap!

My shock was quickly replaced with anger.

Maybe I *was* going to turn back into that creature on the tape. And maybe, once I did, I wouldn't care what happened to the other kids. But as long as I still felt like Todd, I was going to try to *act* like Todd. I was going to make sure Ethan, Jack, and Ashley didn't disappear along with Todd's memories—if it was the last thing I ever did.

I picked up the phone and dialed Ethan's number. The phone rang. Then it rang again.

Come on, Ethan, I thought, *answer the phone.*

Mrs. Rogers picked up the phone. "Hello?" she said, sounding slightly annoyed at having her dinner interrupted once more.

"Mrs. Rogers—" I started, but that was as far as I got. I suddenly discovered that the phone had gone dead in my hands.

At first I thought she'd hung up on me. But then when I couldn't get a dial tone, I realized that the line had been cut. Then the lights went out.

Someone was in the house.

I crept down the stairs as carefully as I could. At the landing I stopped and looked out the window at the street. Sure enough, there was a strange car at the base of the driveway. A beat-up '68 Pontiac. I was certain I'd never seen it before.

I looked over to our next-door neighbour, the Gundersons, a plan forming in my mind. Their lights were on. Instead of waiting for the intruder to come after me and take a chance on ambushing him, I'd slip out the back. I knew the way through the shrubs around our house better than anyone. Or at least Todd did, and thanks to his memories, so did I. Then it was just a matter of asking Mr. Gunderson to call the police.

I crept across the dining room toward the back door. It looked like a short distance to my escape.

But it turned out to be too far.

"Surprise," said a voice behind me in the darkness. Before I could react, a bag was pulled over my head. As I struggled, my hands were duct-taped behind my back. Then something hit me on the back of my skull, and for the second time that day I was unconscious.

Chapter 11

And for the second time that day I woke up in darkness. The truth was, I was starting to get used to it. This time the smell was of motor oil. I was bouncing around a lot. I put two and two together and decided that I was in a trunk—probably the trunk of the Pontiac I'd seen in the street.

One thing was bothering me. Who could be after me now? It wouldn't be the aliens—they thought I was playing on their team. Unless they'd sent someone to check on me, but would an alien drive a junk heap like that Pontiac?

But if it wasn't an alien, who could it be?

After a while the car rolled to a stop. I heard the trunk opening, but I couldn't see a thing since

I was blindfolded. Strong hands lifted me out of the trunk. I tried to say something, but there was tape over my mouth.

Then I was deposited on what felt like a car seat. I heard the trunk close and car doors slam. Then we were moving again.

The blindfold was ripped off my face. I was looking at a tense, muscular man. I recognized him instantly.

"Remember me, Todd?" asked the man behind the wheel.

I nodded.

It was Derek Drennan, the private investigator Don had hired to try to find me. The cold-eyed man from the hospital parking lot. But why was he abducting me? Was he an alien, too—just one who had his game plan confused?

We were on a deserted highway running outside of town. Back in the days when Wisconsin had a mining community, the highway connected boomtowns with the main cities. But those towns, and the people in them, were all dead and gone. I hoped that I wasn't going to join them.

"I'm glad you do remember me, boy," he said. "A memory for faces is important. You've probably figured out by now that I'm a private eye."

His voice was slurred, and I could smell the alcohol on his breath. "I was on your case for nine months, so I've got all the facts on you. And if I know you, Todd, you're probably wondering just what's going on."

He had that right. *Although*, I thought, remembering the scene I'd just witnessed on the videotape from Dr. Strang's office, *there are probably one or two minor facts about me you didn't uncover!*

"Everybody told me you're interested in becoming an investigator yourself. As one detective to another, let me save you some legwork. Here are the facts. Your parents were paying me an awful lot of money to find you. I was making a pretty good living—so long as you were out of the picture." Drennan turned off to the side of the highway and shut off the motor. He turned the headlights off. I hadn't seen another car since he'd removed my blindfold. We were in the middle of nowhere.

"But then you came back suddenly, with no warning. And your parents' money stopped coming. I have to tell you, Todd, it was downright impolite, your coming back like that," he said. "One day I had a good job, and suddenly, the next day I was unemployed.

103

"I don't have to tell you that there's not a whole lot of work for an unemployed private eye in Metier, Wisconsin," he went on. "But do you know what made it really terrible? Your case is still unsolved. The police asked me to open my books after you reappeared. Nine months, I hadn't found a single thing. Not one clue. Not one lead. Not one suspect. Nothing. I'll tell you, Todd, it was embarrassing.

"But then I got to thinking," Drennan continued. "What if you were out of the picture again? What if, somehow, you got kidnapped? I could make a bundle trying to find you—and maybe even collect a little ransom in the bargain!"

I glanced over at the dashboard clock. I was in a serious situation, but now I realized I had even bigger problems than Drennan. The time was eleven-thirty. In a half hour Ethan, Ashley, and Jack would meet by the reservoir. Unless I was there to warn them, no one would ever see them again.

But how was I going to get free?

"You don't seem to be paying attention to me, boy," Drennan said. "You understand what I'm saying? I'm kidnapping you."

My mind raced. I only had one thing to fall back on. If I could transform myself, like I'd done in Dr. Strang's office, getting free would be no problem. But there were two things wrong with that. First, I didn't know how to activate my powers. Second, if I did activate them, would I become a monster—an alien assassin that would be more of a danger to my friends than a help?

But I had no other choice. I had to try.

"That's the problem with you rich kids," Drennan was saying. "You think nothing can touch you." I was concentrating on my hands. If I could just get them to grow, change, morph . . . I strained inside myself, shaking with the effort.

"What's the matter, boy, you scared now?" Drennan asked, noticing how I shook. "You want to say something to me now?"

There. I felt it. A heat that started in my head and spread out to the rest of my body. It was my power. I was certain of it. It was waiting for me.

"Well, what do you have to say for yourself, Mr. Rich Kid?" Drennan asked, and ripped the tape from my mouth.

I stared at my kidnapper. Suddenly he seemed very small. I looked at him the way a cat looks at a mouse. From his expression I knew what he was looking back at.

I knew I had no eyes.

"Boy," I said, "did you pick the wrong guy on the wrong day."

The power hit my body like a wave of raw heat. My already torn clothes now burst like the Incredible Hulk's. I swelled in every direction. The seat belt buckle blew apart with a loud *pang!* My arms rippled with muscles like two thick steel cables.

Drennan's mouth hung open in fear.

"I have three words for you," I hissed, *"change of plans.* From here on in, *I'm* kidnapping *you."*

Before he could scream, I brought my elbow up hard and fast, catching him neatly under the chin. Then as his head rolled backward I brought my forehead sharply against his—*head butt time!* He went out like a match hitting water. A few minutes later he was in the trunk, lying just where I'd been a few minutes before.

How quickly the tables turned! The night was turning out better than I expected.

Drennan's long khaki overcoat was lying in the front seat. I tossed it on over my shredded clothes, then climbed in the car.

Twenty-five minutes to go. And two new problems:

Not only wasn't I sure where I was heading, I wasn't sure how to drive.

_____ **Chapter 12**

Manoeuvering the big car turned out to be easier than I thought. Then I remembered: I wasn't really a thirteen-year-old kid. I was an alien assassin, undoubtedly trained in hundreds of different skills. Hadn't I driven Dr. Strang's car to the mall earlier? If I had a plane instead of a car, I realized, I could probably fly it.

Through an obstacle course.

But I would have to be careful with my new skills. The more I explored who I had been before I became Todd, the more that side might come out. I had seen the evil inside me. I wanted it as far away as possible. I had to keep the Todd part of me in control.

Suddenly I really wished I'd finished reading

Dr. Jekyll and Mr. Hyde. I wanted to know how it ends.

I sped along the road back into town. I checked my reflection in the rearview mirror and was startled to see Derek Drennan staring back at me! Apparently I had shape-shifted into his body without even realizing it. What else was the alien inside me doing without my realizing it?

Speeding, it turned out. The answer came to me in a burst of blue-and-red lights as a patrol car came into view in my rearview mirror. Municipal code 40:17, section 2, set the speed limit outside Metier city limits at fifty miles per hour. I'd been doing closer to eighty. The police cruiser looked huge behind me. It was time to pull over.

The man who got out of the cruiser looked almost too young to be a police officer. He must be new to the force—I'd never seen him before in all the times I hung around the police station. A glance at his car confirmed my suspicions: it was empty. He hadn't even been assigned a partner yet.

I had heard enough stories from police officers about what to do and what not to do when pulled over for speeding. For one thing, I knew not to try to talk my way out of it. That would only make things worse. *Besides*, I realized, *it's not like I'm going to be around to pay for the ticket.*

If I just kept calm, I'd be out of this situation in no time. But I felt a slight prickling at the back of my neck. *Must not stop*, said a voice inside me. *Must attack. Eliminate the human.*

I was going to get myself shot! I gripped the hand rest and got myself under control as the patrolman walked up to my window, shining his flashlight in my eyes. I smiled as politely as I could, Derek Drennan's big face feeling awkward on my head. The officer's badge read *Wyzkowski*.

"Good evening, Officer," I said. My voice was that of an adult man's. I could hardly believe how deep and low it sounded! "Was I speeding?"

"That's a fifty-mile-an-hour zone back there," he said.

"Yes, I know," I said. "Municipal code 40:17, section 2."

"That's right," he said. Then he reconsidered. "Are you trying to get smart with me?" he demanded.

"Not at all, Officer," I said. "I just wanted to let you know that I know the law. And I'm sorry. I just wasn't thinking."

"Well, what got you going in such a hurry?" he asked.

I thought for a moment, fishing for a plausible lie. Then I remembered: *Just tell him the truth and get back on the road.* "The truth is, Officer," I said, "I'm just late to meet some friends."

That satisfied him. He relaxed. "Well, I can understand that, but the law's the law."

"Of course," I said.

"License and registration, please."

I felt the cold needles of panic. License! I didn't have a license! If I told him I didn't have one on me, he might tow the car and take me to the station! I didn't have time for this—and I wasn't sure how long I could pass as someone twenty years older than my actual age.

Then suddenly I felt my hand pull toward one side. What was going on? Against my will my right hand started crawling across my lap like a flesh-colored crab. It crawled inside Drennan's coat, settling on my pants pocket. The index finger tapped twice on something hard inside the pocket.

Had I lost control of my own body?

"Just a moment, Officer," I said. I reached into the pocket and pulled out . . . Drennan's wallet!

110

The assassin part of me must have known I might need it and taken it from the unconscious private detective's pocket.

Well, at least we were working as a team. I shuddered, wondering what was going to happen when I no longer wanted to play along.

I handed the patrolman the two cards. He studied them closely. "I'll tell you what, Mr. Drennan," he said. "If I wrote you out a ticket, it'd take fifteen minutes and then you'd really be late to see those friends. So I'll let you go. But you just think about what might have happened here."

"Yes, Officer," I said. "I'm certainly grateful."

He smiled. "Drive safe, then," he said.

That was when I heard the noise. A loud *thump-thump- thump!* that stood out in the silence of the abandoned highway like a neon sign.

It was coming from the trunk. Had Officer Wyzkowski heard it as well? I didn't have to wonder for very long.

"What was that?" the policeman asked, pointing his flashlight toward the trunk.

How was I going to explain this one?

The assassin inside me panicked. *Kill him!* it shouted. *Jump him! Grab him!* I tightened my grip on the hand rest, clenching my teeth, fighting for control over the creature.

"Noth-nothing, Officer," I stammered.

"Is that so?" He peered into the car. I tried to grin, feebly. "You look a little nervous there, Mr. Drennan. You want to step out of the car?"

"Sure," I said. "No problem."

"Slowly," he said, backing away. "Let me see both your hands."

As I stepped from the car, a low moan came from the trunk. "What's in there?" Wyzkowski demanded. "Have you got someone in your trunk?"

"No, Officer," I lied.

"Are you trying to tell me that wasn't a human being that just made that noise? Well, let's have a look," he said. "Give me the keys."

More thrashing was heard from the closed compartment. Drennan sounded about ready to get up and go jogging. He must have had a head like a concrete brick!

"Officer Wyzkowski," I started, trying to retain my rapidly slipping grip on the situation, "for your own safety, I'm asking you—"

"I said, give me the keys," he barked. "Now! Do it!"

I handed him the keys. Even as I did so, I could feel the alien taking over, stretching, growing. The ground was suddenly farther away.

The officer bent over the trunk, trying to turn the key in the lock. I watched as the skin grew silvery on my arms—if you could still call them arms. They were becoming long and angular, the fingers sharp and clawlike.

I looked at the back of Officer Wyskowski's head. If I made it quick and painless, he might not feel anything until he woke up the next morning.

The trunk opened with a pop. "What the—!" Officer Wyzkowski said, looking at Drennan's hog-tied form.

"If you like that," I hissed, my huge claws gleaming in the moonlight like two rows of knives, "you're gonna love this."

Moments later I found myself speeding along the highway back into town. I was going well over a hundred miles per hour. But this time there was no question of being pulled over.

This time I was in a police cruiser, with the lights and siren going full blast. Officer Wyzkowski's uniform turned out to be a perfect fit—not surprising, since I now looked like I could be his twin. I was really getting the hang of this shape-shifting thing. But that's what worried me.

The monster had almost gained control. Nothing brought it out like a good fight—even if the poor police officer wasn't able to put up much resistance. It could have taken over then. But it made a mistake when it had me slide behind the wheel of the patrol car.

I had dreamed my entire life of sitting right where I was sitting now, in the driver's seat of a police cruiser—or Todd had, anyway. There was no way he was going to miss this moment.

Thanks to Todd, I knew the workings of the police car inside out. It was easy to call in over the police radio and explain where we'd been—Todd knew exactly what to say.

"Calling dispatch," I barked into the car radio. "Dispatch, do you read? Over."

"This is dispatch," a voice on the other end of the radio said. "Say your forty."

"Say your forty"—that was police talk for, "Tell me who you are and where you are." I checked the vehicle identification number under the dash.

"This is car eleven," I radioed back. "I'm on the old service road outside of town."

"Do you have a situation, car eleven?" the dispatcher asked, meaning, "Are you in trouble?"

"That's a negative," I replied. "I came out on a goose chase. Someone saw a couple of"—I remembered the dream—"teenagers with bad attitudes."

"Yep. They're probably the ones responsible for the graffiti at the high school," the dispatcher said. "That big sign that says UFOs Land Here."

"Could be," I told him. "Listen, I'm going to lay low for a while, see what I can see."

"Do you want backup?" he asked.

"No," I said. "I think I can handle a couple of kids myself. Don't send anyone else. In fact, why don't you tell the other cars to just steer clear of me. I don't want to attract any attention."

"Copy that," the dispatcher said, police talk for yes. "Go get 'em, car eleven. Over and out."

"Out," I replied. The radio went dead.

I looked into the rearview mirror. The face of Officer Wyzkowski looked back at me through Todd's eyes. I smiled. This might be my last night on earth, but at least I'd made it on to the force before I left—a full five years ahead of schedule.

But as I sped forward on my mission I realized it wouldn't be so easy to hold on to my identity. Already I was finding it harder and harder to think of myself as Todd Aldridge. A part of me was actually looking forward to seeing the mother ship, the rendezvous, the victory. A part of me saw the lights of the town up ahead not as Metier, my hometown, but as an enormous landing strip. A part of me was looking forward to seeing the earthlings fail.

That was a part of me that I had to fight.

And I would fight. But it was going to be up-hill all the way.

Before I knew it, I was back in town. I pulled onto the familiar main street. My head was pounding as if it were going to split in half. The clock in the dashboard read 11:45. I struggled to keep control.

I concentrated, thinking Todd thoughts. I held on to the sights and sounds of the quiet town like a ship holds onto an anchor. There was the little bakery where Todd got his twelfth birthday cake. No, I thought, not "where Todd got his cake." Where *I* got *my* cake. I had to think that way, or I'd be lost forever.

There was the drugstore where his mom—*my*

mom—used to go in the middle of the night to get medicine for *my* earaches. There was the video store with its rows of video game cartridges: I knew them all by heart. A display in the window announced the arrival of the latest version of Tomb Raider, *my* all-time favourite.

There was the pet store where I had bought Max. I peered closely at the window as it passed. Sure enough, there was a trio of beagle puppies in the display, two asleep and one jumping at its own reflection.

I rolled to a halt in front of a stoplight. I had shut my red-and-blue emergency lights off when I entered town. I was in a hurry, but there was no need to attract additional attention. Some officer might spot me and decide that I could use some backup—just what I didn't need.

As I watched the billboard over Metier Memorial Bank it began to melt and change. The faces of the people in the ad looked different somehow. It took me a moment to realize what was different. They had no eyes, just black disks.

Then I looked at the Walk/Don't Walk sign, willing the light to change. I had to get out of there. But the sign had altered. Instead of reading *Don't Walk*, it blinked:

DON'T
FAIL.

I was slipping. The alien was coming through. I had to keep my eyes on the road and my mind on Todd.

I was in for a fight. With myself.

Chapter 13

Just as the dashboard clock in the patrol car hit five to midnight I screamed up in front of the reservoir. My head hurt even more than before. It was as if the alien were trying to claw its way out the top of my skull.

I yanked open the door of the big cruiser and hit the ground running. There was the hole in the storm fence, just like I remembered it. I ducked under it, never slowing my pace. I wondered if I was too late.

It turned out to be a mistake—a big mistake. I'd forgotten that I was still in the body of Officer Wyzkowski, and Officer Wyzkowski was at least a foot taller than Todd Aldridge. The ragged edges of the chain-link fence scraped across my neck and back, tearing huge rents in my police uniform.

I bit my lip, trying to hold back the pain. I reached one hand up to free my collar from the steel grip of the fence. It came back wet and sticky. I looked at it under the moonlight. The blood was silver, just as it had been that afternoon.

I wasn't Todd Aldridge. I wasn't human. I didn't know what I was.

I felt my features stretch and pull. *No,* I screamed, silently, *this can't be happening!*

"Todd," a familiar voice commanded, "don't resist me. You can't win. You can't hide from who you are."

I suddenly realized where I'd heard that voice before. On Dr. Strang's videotape. Only now it was coming out of my own mouth.

The skin on my hands began to turn silvery and pale, like the alien's I'd seen in the tape. My muscles continued their painful morphing. The alien was right. I couldn't hide behind Todd anymore. I couldn't run away from who I was.

"I may not be able to change who I am," I growled back at the alien intruder, my teeth gritted in tight concentration, "but I can decide what I'm going to do."

Focusing all my energies in my hands, I slowly, inch by inch, began to push the assassin out. The "Mr. Hyde" in me didn't want to go—but my "Dr. Jekyll" was still stronger.

Finally I was in the body of Todd Aldridge again. A normal-looking thirteen-year-old boy. With normal-looking skin.

Trouble was, I had a good quarter mile to run—in a police uniform fifteen sizes too big for me. I kicked off the big black shoes, hitched up the thick blue trousers, and began to run, barefoot, through the marsh that surrounded the reservoir.

At first I thought I was too late. The reservoir was dead quiet. I saw no sign of the other kids.

Had the aliens come early and abducted Jack, Ethan, and Ashley already? Was I too late? Had I failed?

Just as I felt my hopes falling I heard a faint voice calling me from the bushes. "Todd," it called. It was Ethan! "We're over here."

I ran over to the bushes where the three teenagers had concealed themselves. The dense leaves provided excellent cover. "We were afraid you weren't coming," said Ethan.

"We saw you run over," Ashley continued, "but . . . we weren't sure it was you."

What did she mean by that? Had they seen me start to transform into the assassin? In a flash I realized: If they knew the truth about me, they might not listen to anything I had to say. The truth was, if the positions were reversed, *I* wouldn't listen to me, either.

But if they didn't believe me, I wouldn't be able to save them. I had to convince them I was Todd at all costs.

"Yeah, Todd." Jack laughed. "I know I'm not as snappy a dresser as you are, but still—what's with the costume?"

"The costume?" I asked. Oh—they were only talking about the police uniform! In my desperate effort to concentrate on being Todd, I'd totally forgotten what I was wearing. "Sorry, Jack," I said. "I know how much you like my suit, but it's at the cleaners'."

"You know," Ashley said, "I've seen *Lethal Weapon* twenty times, and that looks almost like a *real* police outfit."

"It is," I said, "it is a real police outfit. But look, I'll explain it later, okay? We have more important things to worry about."

"Such as what?" Ashley wanted to know. "You're acting very strange, Todd."

"Come on, Ashley, the guy's been on an alien ship for nine months," Ethan said. "Cut him a little—"

"We're in terrible danger," I interrupted. "The alien mother ship is going to land right here in a matter of minutes. We have to get to safety."

"I don't understand," Ashley said. "How do you know about this? And why did you ask us to come out to the reservoir at midnight if this is where the aliens are going to land?"

"I'll explain," I said, desperately scanning the skies. How much more time remained before the clouds started to whirl and our time ran out? "I'll explain all of that. But for now you have to trust me. We have to get out of here."

"We should listen to him," Ethan said.

"I don't know, Ethan," Jack said. "The assassins can change their shapes. What if he's not the real Todd Aldridge?"

"Please!" I said. "You have to believe me! By the time I convince you I'm who I say I am, we're all going to be dead!"

"I've never heard an alien say please before,"

Ethan said. "That's proof enough for me. Let's go."

Reluctantly Jack and Ashley emerged behind Ethan from their hiding place.

"Better safe than sorry," Ashley said.

"Yeah, and better sorry than dead," Jack said. "But Todd, promise you'll explain all of this later."

No! a voice inside me screamed. *Don't let them leave! Stop them! They must be at the reservoir when the mother ship lands!*

"I promise," I said. "Let's go."

I started up the embankment. Each step was a trial, as the alien inside me fought me all the way. My legs felt like lead. *Must stop the humans! Must not fail!* the voice shrieked. *Cannot fail! Must . . . win!* I wanted to clamp my hands over my ears—but I didn't think that would help make the others less suspicious of me.

As we reached the police cruiser I snuck a peek at the clock on the dashboard. One minute to midnight. I looked up at the skies. So far, they were quiet.

Too quiet.

"A police car?" Ashley asked, looking at the black-and-white vehicle incredulously. "First that uniform and now an actual police car? How did you get it, Todd?"

"I'm, uh, pretty close with a guy on the force," I said, patting the trunk where Officer Wyzkowski lay tied up in his underwear. *Yeah, pretty close*, I thought, *like six inches away*.

"Todd," Jack said, "have you ever thought you might be taking this law enforcement hobby a little too far?"

"How are we going to get out of here?" Ethan asked. "Can you drive?"

"Sure, I can drive," I said. All the while the alien was frantically trying to gain control. It felt like he was throwing himself against the walls of my skull, body-slamming the interior of my cranium. I concentrated on the sound of my heart beating. How much time did I have left? "Come on," I said. "There's no time to talk! Just get in the car!"

They had started to board the vehicle when suddenly Jack froze, one hand on the door handle.

"Oh, my God," he said, barely breathing.

"What?" I asked, instinctively scanning the skies for the mother ship.

"Ethan . . . his eyes," Jack said. "Look at his eyes!"

"What about my eyes?" I asked, but as soon as the question left my lips I knew what he was talking about.

I crouched to check my reflection in the side-view mirror.

The alien had the last laugh after all.

Chapter 14

In my reflection in the side-view mirror I could see that my eyes were now two black disks.

"You're . . . you're . . . ," Ethan said, stepping away from the car.

"I *knew it*," Ashley said.

"No! Guys! You don't understand!" I yelled. I was so close! If I could only make them listen to me, I could drive them to safety. I could save their lives. I could—

"Run," Jack screamed to the others. "Follow me!"

He dashed under the fence, then tore down the path back toward the reservoir. Ethan and Ashley followed close on his heels.

They were all going to be killed—and there

was nothing I could do to save them. Nothing except run.

I leaped out of the police car and hauled butt after them, running as fast as I could over the brambles and damp leaves. The cool April air tore at my lungs. Sharp rocks hurt my bare feet.

"Wait!" I yelled between gasps. "The mother ship . . . it's coming. . . ."

"What mother ship, liar!" Jack shouted over his shoulder. He was far ahead of me now. There was no way I'd catch up. "The sky is clear!"

I had no good answer for that, but I knew I had to catch him. I felt my legs stretch and expand. The skin on my arms went silvery-gray.

I was an alien once again.

And I was a wicked fast alien at that.

Suddenly the distance between me and the three fleeing teenagers started to close. Running them down would be easy. I felt no difficulty, no strain; my legs hammered the ground effortlessly as I soared through the night air. If the guys on the track team could only see me now, I thought.

I lashed out with one hand and caught Ethan

around the ankle. He fell to the mud, sprawling. "Ethan," I said, "you've got to listen to me—"

When he turned over, his face was full of fear—and anger. He seemed transformed. His eyes literally seemed to glow in the darkness. "Sorry, Todd," he said, "or whoever you are. The time for listening is over." He pulled back his fist, aiming for my throat.

But just as he was going to deal me a blow that would surely have left me unconscious, a low rumbling sound came over the surface of the reservoir. Ethan made a small noise, craning his head to see. The noise seemed to come from beneath us, from under the swamp itself.

"What was that?" Ethan asked.

As if in answer, thousands of tons of steel emerged all at once from under the water of the reservoir! It rose into sight like a giant silver beetle. An enormous glowing orb of metal and crystal was suddenly hanging in the air above the lake, spectacularly beautiful—if it wasn't so deadly.

I knew immediately that it was the mother ship. The alien part of me grew delirious with excitement. *Soon*, it thought, *victory will be ours! The earthlings could not have gone far! Our mission will be a success!*

I seized the moment of surprise to flip Ethan onto his stomach. I locked his arms behind his neck, neutralizing him. A plan was forming in the Todd-part of my mind—but if it was going to work, I'd need to be free of interruptions.

The ship's bulkhead struck the bank of the reservoir, sending a shock wave tremor through the ground. An enormous plume of steam shot out of what I knew was an exit hatch. Blue electricity arced from the smooth metal of the ship through the cool spring night air.

A massive metal plank emerged from the glowing hatch, slowly expanding, reaching, like an insect's feeler. It was the ship's gangway—an incredibly advanced staircase that could be assembled or dismantled anywhere, in any environment, to allow the aliens to descend from their ship. It could even be lowered while the ship was in motion in case of an emergency, and special stabilizers would permit the assassins to walk down it as safely as if it were in an enclosed building.

Two of my "comrades in arms"—tall, silvery pale aliens with bulbous heads and large black eyes—stepped down the gangway and leaped gingerly, like big cats, to the ground. Immediately they spotted me and hurried over.

The alien in me thrilled to see its plan falling into place. The Todd part of me knew that the next few minutes would determine whether I'd succeed in saving Ethan, Ashley, and Jack.

"Excellent work," the first alien hissed at me, "excellent. Our leader will be pleased. Where are the others?"

It was now or never.

"That way," I said. "They took a vehicle toward the main road. If you hurry, you can catch them!"

The two nodded and ran off the way I'd pointed—in the wrong direction!

"You—you pointed the wrong way!" Ethan said from his position on the ground. "What's going on? Who are you really?"

"I'm an assassin, just like the others," I hissed. "My body is, anyway."

"Then why did you just help my friends escape?" he asked.

"Because when they programmed me, they screwed up," I said. "They figured that giving

131

me Todd Aldridge's memories would make my disguise foolproof. But the Todd part is stronger than they think. It's like they gave me more than his memories, they gave me his conscience . . . his soul."

With my acute alien hearing, I could hear the two aliens running up the ridge to where the police cruiser was parked. I knew they'd be back soon. We didn't have much time.

"They'll be returning any second now," I told Ethan, "just as soon as they find that Jack and Ashley aren't up there."

Ethan got to his feet. "What are we going to do?" he asked. "How am I going to get away? Do you have a plan?"

I smiled. It was a smile of regret. What I was about to do would seal my fate.

"I've got a plan," I said abruptly. "You don't escape."

"What?" Ethan cried. "But you just said you'd help me!"

"Be quiet," I warned, "or they'll hear us talking. Listen. Here's what we're going to do."

The two aliens returned from over the ridge. They came sliding down the muddy trail to the banks of the reservoir lake, stopping at Ethan's prone body.

"You!" one said, prodding him with a toe. "Where is your captor?"

The boy said nothing.

"Are you deaf?" the second one hissed. "Where is the one who captured you? And where did your friends go? Tell us, and we may spare your life."

The teenager groaned and tried weakly to turn over but collapsed in the mud.

"They must have fought," the first alien said. "The boy looks badly beaten."

"He must talk! He must tell us how to find the others!" the second alien growled.

"He cannot talk," the first alien replied, "and we are out of time. We must leave, or we will miss our rendezvous. And if that happens . . ."

"If that happens, our leader will be displeased," the second alien agreed.

"Besides," the first alien hissed, "this one is Henley's son."

"Yes," the second alien agreed. "Now that we have him, we can depart with honour. Help me with the boy's body."

Slowly they dragged the boy toward the glowing hull of the ship, then carried him up the gangway. Once inside, they placed their captive inside a large plastic tube that ran from the floor to the ceiling. It held his unconscious form in a standing position.

Only when the aliens had begun the blastoff procedure did he open his eyes.

They were two black disks.

My eyes.

I had managed one final shape-shift.

I regarded Ethan's reflection in the curved plastic of the tube. The aliens had fallen for it. I watch Ethan's mouth—my mouth—twist into a satisfied smile.

"Command one, this is the mother ship," the first alien hissed into a console. "We have captured the first target. We are returning to the rendezvous point."

"What is the status of Agent Cynor?" a voice crackled over the intercom.

"Cynor . . . has been left behind," the second alien said. If I hadn't known better, I would have sworn there was a touch of regret in his voice.

Cynor. So that was my name. I wondered what else I was going to learn about myself in the days to come.

Somewhere down below us Ethan was probably running after Jack and Ashley in a too loose policeman's uniform. He'd have quite a story to tell them. I hoped that he'd make it. Part of me knew that he would.

And if he didn't, I'd just have to come back and save his butt all over again.

About the Author

Chris Archer grew up in New Jersey, where he spent most of his childhood wishing he had special powers.

He now divides his time between New York City and Los Angeles, California. When Chris is not writing books and screenplays, he enjoys going to scary movies, playing piano (badly), and reading suspense novels.

He has never been to Wisconsin.

What shocking power do you possess?
The answer could warp your mind . . .

Don't miss

MINDWARP

ALIEN IMPOSTOR

Did you ever give someone a shock? You
know – run your bare hand feet across the
carpet and touch someone's hand? That's
nothing compared to what I can do.

You see, ever since my thirteenth birthday,
I've been able to control electricity.
Appliances, video games . . . any kind of
electrical device at all is suddenly under
my command. I can even make lightning.
Cool, right?

Wrong.

Because now something is after me.
A horrible creature that wants to shut off
my power for good.

Mindwarp

Chris Archer

❏	0 340 71645 2	Alien Terror	£3.99
❏	0 340 71646 0	Alien Blood	£3.99
❏	0 340 71647 9	Alien Scream	£3.99
❏	0 340 71648 7	Alien Sight	£3.99
❏	0 340 71649 5	Alien Impostor	£3.99
❏	0 340 71650 9	Alien Shock	£3.99

All Hodder Children's books are available at your local bookshop, or can be ordered direct from the publisher. Just tick the titles you would like and complete the details below. Prices and availability are subject to change without prior notice.

Please enclose a cheque or postal order made payable to *Bookpoint Ltd*, and send to: Hodder Children's Books, 39 Milton Park, Abingdon, OXON OX14 4TD, UK.
Email Address: orders@bookpoint.co.uk

TITLE		FIRST NAME		SURNAME	
ADDRESS					
DAYTIME TEL:			POST CODE		

If you would prefer to pay by credit card, please complete:
Please debit my Visa/Access/Diner's Card/American Express (delete as applicable) card no:

Signature ....

Expiry Date: ....

Alternatively, our call centre team would be delighted to take your order by telephone if you would like to pay by credit card. Our direct line is *01235 400414* (lines open 9.00 am–6.00 pm Monday to Saturday, 24 hour message answering service.) or you could send a fax on *01235 400454*.

If you would NOT like to receive further information on our products please tick the box. ❏